THE ORACLE

THE ORACLE

By

Frank F. Fiore

"With all due affection to Ray Bradbury"

AUTHOR'S NOTE

Years ago, I read many a book by authors of the Golden Age of Science Fiction. One such book was *The Illustrated Man* by Ray Bradbury – a very different adventure in reading.

Bradbury certainly found an original way to present a collection of short stories - a series of stories within a larger story. So, I decided to take a leaf out of *The Illustrated Man* and write a book of Sci-Fi short stories in this Bradbury style.

If you like tales with a twist at the end in the vein of the Twilight Zone episodes and the short stories of Jeffrey Archer, then you should enjoy these entertaining flights into the imaginary.

If you do, please write a review of THE ORACLE on Amazon. I would greatly appreciate it.

See more of what I've written at my author site www.frankfiore.com and if you want to stay up to date on new stories written by me, subscribe to my *Frank Remarks* newsletter. Email me at frank@frankfiore.com and put the word SUBSCRIBE in the subject line.

Enjoy.

THE ORACLE

It was a gradual thing. So slow that I hadn't noticed anything was wrong until I heard the steady staccato sound of what could only be one thing-the tread of the recapped tire I'd just bought that morning in Los Angeles, peeling off.

I grabbed the wheel tightly. There was a sudden muted thud as the tire disintegrated and the car pulled to the right. My high school Drivers Ed flashed through my mind—steer into the skid or opposite? Screw it! I took my foot off the gas and battled the car to a stop on the shoulder of the road.

I climbed out of the car, a classic 1965 Chevy Corvair that Vince, my on again, off again manager, had loaned me. He couldn't lend me a newer one because he didn't own a newer car – well, at least anything that you would consider a recent model. Vince collected classic cars and didn't own any other type.

The Chevy Corvair was definitely a classic. It had enjoyed only a limited manufacturing run that was cut short by the consumer advocate, Ralph Nader, who had labeled the Corvair unsafe at any speed.

Hmm...I wonder if Vince had loaned me this particular car on purpose? I thought about the insurance policy he made me take out before the trip. He was a sleaze, but ...nah.

Accepting my fate, I walked around the car to the passenger side and stared at the rear tire. "Damn." Not only had the tread peeled off, but the sidewalls had shredded as well. There basically wasn't anything left of it.

A quick look around told me I needed to hurry and get it changed. There was a storm to the west. The same storm I'd outrun when I left L.A. earlier.

Popping the hood - and yes, I did know the Corvair's engine was in the back - I began digging through my luggage, removing my backpack and electric guitar before I found the spare tire buried in the usual place at the bottom of the trunk.

"Shit!" I screamed to no one in particular. The spare was flat!

I should have known Vince wouldn't have bothered to maintain it. But I was in a hurry and didn't stop to think about it.

As I stood shaking my head and cussing, I realized that even if the spare was good, I couldn't have changed the tire.

Double shit! No jack!

I surveyed the area and realized I was in trouble. The place where the tire decided to take a crap on me was desolate. I couldn't see anything in any direction. Then I remembered, some time back, maybe twenty miles, I'd seen a sign that said, "Next gas and service-sixty miles".

I stacked my stuff back under the hood, slammed it down, and went to sit in the driver's seat. I leaned over and opened the glove box and found the tattered map of Arizona. I tucked it in there at the start of my trip along with the directions to the Lollapalooza audition Vince had arranged for me. He said it could be my big break - and besides, he needed the money I'd bring in if I got the gig. I saw it as a chance to take a break from the L.A. scene.

Checking the map, I figured I was about fifty miles south of Kingman, and then I remembered passing a sign for Wikieup a few miles back. I decided that was my best shot, so I decided to walk, hoping to meet up with a Good Samaritan on the road who'd give me a ride to the nearest town.

I wasn't too confident, though, that I'd catch a ride anytime soon. I was dressed in faded jeans and a Megadeth t-shirt. I had long hair halfway down my back, tied in a ponytail. I had a cheap backpack that I had bought a few years ago, when I thought I was going to college - it also a big Megadeth logo on it. I slung the backpack over one shoulder and my electric guitar in its leather carrying case over the other. I didn't exactly blend in with the natives, plus I hadn't seen a car for the last couple of hours.

So I walked and I walked and I walked.

The whole time, the squall I'd outrun earlier was steadily catching up. Even though it was still early, not quite four in the afternoon, the storm clouds had already obscured the sun to the point that it looked and felt as though it were twilight.

As I strode on, I could hear the steady increase in the telltale rumbling of the thunder. I could feel the humidity climbing and could see the rain in the distance across the high desert. The wind blew with the smell of wet mesquite.

This was not the place I wanted to be, out in the open, when the storm finally hit. It had all the earmarks of being a torrential downpour and that would mean possible flash floods and lightning strikes.

Off in the distance, on the side of a hill, I saw an old ranch house. There was a long access road that led to it, which appeared to have been used regularly and recently. So I began trotting down the road in the hopes of outrunning the approaching storm.

As I jogged up to the house, I was reminded of the ranches I'd seen in the old westerns on TV. The home was a long ranch-style affair with a few cottonwood trees off to the left of it. There was a big, rundown barn off to the right of the dwelling with a large empty corral next to it. The portrait of the Old West was completed by the purple mountains in the background and the thunderstorm rolling in over the top of them—like a Remington painting—one I wished I wasn't in.

I jogged to the ranch house and up the two steps to the dilapidated porch just as the first heavy raindrops began to fall. I was about to open the tattered screen door, then thought better of it and just knocked on the weathered front door through the torn screen.

As the rain began to come down in earnest, I knocked a second time. As I waited for a response, I hugged the wall of the ranch house in an attempt to stay dry, because the wind had picked up and was blowing the rain onto the porch.

After a minute or two no one answered the door, so I knocked a third time.

I was beginning to think there was no one home, or the place was deserted. So I leaned over to look in a window and thought I heard the creaking of the front door as it opened. Someone was peering out though the small opening between the door and its jamb.

"Oh! Hi there." I spoke, sounding as friendly as possible. "My car broke down a few miles up the road. It's got a flat and I don't have a spare." I informed the mystery person.

Slowly the door opened wider, revealing a tall, craggy old man with an apprehensive look on his face. He eyed me suspiciously from beneath a tuft of white hair and then looked around the immediate area as though he wasn't convinced by my story. Probably looking for a hippie convoy of my pals.

"I'd appreciate being able to use your phone to call for a tow." I said.

"Haven't got one." He croaked as he stared through me.

I got the distinct impression he was giving me the once over, trying to decide whether I was worth any more of his time. I was starting to get a bit unnerved by his glare when I heard a voice from inside the house call out.

"Jeb, who's at the door?" It was a woman's voice.

The man turned slightly towards the voice as an elderly woman stepped up, opened the door wide and said, "Come on in young man, It's not fitting to be standing outside in weather like this."

She gave the old man a hard look. "Where are your manners, Jeb?" she admonished.

As I stepped inside, the woman asked. "Is there something we can help you with, young man? We don't get to see visitors out here unless they've had some sort of car trouble."

"That's exactly what happened. The car I borrowed from a friend had a flat tire and when I went to put on the spare I found it was flat. I could sure use a ride to the nearest town so I could arrange to have it towed in and the spare tire fixed."

"Oh my, that certainly is a problem, but I'm afraid we won't be able to get you into town tonight," the woman stated casually.

"Oh, why?" I asked.

"The storm of course. The National Weather Service has issued a flash flood warning and that's something we take very seriously around here. "Right, Jeb?" she stated, as she elbowed him in the ribs.

The poke seemed to work on old Jeb. He spoke up quickly. "Yeah, right." He coughed out the words in a raspy voice.

The old woman gave him a look that would have made most men cringe, but not old Jeb. He just turned and walked into the living room.

"You can set your things down right here and then go take a seat in the living room. Are you hungry? I was just about to put dinner on the table and there is plenty to go around," she offered.

"Well now that you mention it, I haven't eaten all day."

"Good. It'll be just a few minutes and dinner will be served. We haven't had a guest for dinner in a very long time," she stated as she turned and walked into what I assumed was the kitchen.

As I wandered into the living room, Jeb glanced at me for only a moment. I could tell even though he wasn't all that comfortable with my sudden arrival along with the storm, he would allow me to stay. I guess he'd learned long ago that it was easier to let his wife have things her way than to fight about it. That's the kind of wisdom that takes us men years to come to terms with, my dad used to say.

As I sat on the sofa and looked at the pictures of the two of them on the walls, I noticed the striking contrast between my two guests. Whereas Jeb was tall and lanky, she was short and stocky. Whereas Jeb was a bit standoffish, she was warm and friendly, perhaps even caring. Jeb's features were weathered and gray. Hers were soft and silvery, sort of grandmotherly.

You could tell from his looks, Jeb had never had a desk job and she had most likely never worked outside their home. They were both at least in their seventies, but they might have been even older-though they both appeared to still be spry and vibrant.

Jeb sat in what, I was sure, his special recliner across from the sofa. He picked up the newspaper from the table next to him and began reading-ignoring me.

So I spent my time checking out the room some more. They had good taste as far as I could see. There were Navajo rugs on the floor and Mexican clay pots filled with flowers in the corners of the room. The furniture had a Santa Fe look to it. It was white pine and hefty. The walls, I noticed, were covered with pictures and mixed in with ones of the two of them at different places, were several assorted scenes from the Old West. On the wall hung a 1982 Farmers Insurance calendar – the kind insurance agents give you for the next year.

I was about to ask Jeb about the pictures when his wife strolled into the room.

"I must be slipping. How impolite of me. We never even introduced ourselves or asked your name," she stated, as she stepped over next to Jeb.

"I'm Chris." I said.

"And I'm Helen and this, of course, is, Jeb," she stated.

"It's good to meet you", I replied. Helen nudged Jeb and he made a grumbling sound from behind the newspaper.

"You'll have to excuse the old man here. He's become quite the loner in his old age. If he could he'd probably have me only come

around at feeding time. He's like an old crotchety bear," she stated, as Jeb growled again from behind the newspaper.

"Now you're welcome to stay the night, Chris. We have a spare room all decked out and it would be inhuman to turn someone out on a night like this." The lightning flashed and the thunder crashed at that precise moment as if to emphasize her point.

"Oh no, that's not necessary," I replied.

"Nonsense, what are you going to do? Sleep out in a puddle?" she asked. "We can't take you to town until tomorrow sometime because of the storm, remember?"

"Oh yeah, I a... just didn't want to be an inconvenience."

"It's no problem. Jeb and I are happy to help others in need," she said. She turned and walked out of the room bubbling over her shoulder, "Dinner will be ready in about ten minutes, boys. Jeb, why don't you be just a bit more sociable and entertain our guest while I finish up in here."

Jeb, as if on cue, set down the paper, glanced towards the kitchen, grumbled something incoherent, and then looked over at me. "Do ya like pictures?" he asked with a slight twinkle in his eyes.

"Sure, I guess. What kind are we talking about?" I asked. From the change in his expression of one of disinterest to one of almost devious, pictures of 1940s porn raced through my mind. I became even more uncomfortable.

He leaned forward in his chair, as if he were sharing a secret. "Three D pictures," he said. He reached into a battered cardboard box beside his chair and pulled out an old time stereoscopic slide viewer. It was a stereopticon made of wood, about twelve inches long, with a viewer on one end that looked like a diver's mask that fit over the viewer's eyes. On the other end was the slide holder that slid back and forth to focus the 3D images.

Being a catalogue junkie, I'd seen one or two before. They were the 19th century's equivalent of today's VCR. At least one of these entertainment devices was found in nearly every middle and upper class parlor of that time period.

"Ever see one of these?" Jeb asked.

"I've seen pictures of them, but never an actual one."

"I got this one for Helen on our wedding anniversary. Thought it would be nice to have it since it was an antique and all." His eyes went to the coffee table in front of me. "Hand me that box under the table there."

I looked down and saw a small silver colored metal box on the lower shelf. It was three inches by five inches and had a smooth finish, with no exterior markings.

I pulled it out and handed it to Jeb, who slipped the top off and set it on the table next to him. He gently pulled a slide from inside the box.

As he slid the small transparency into the stereopticon in his hand he asked, "Married?"

"What?" I wasn't sure I heard him correctly. I was so focused on watching how gently he was loading the slide into the viewer.

"Are you married, boy?" Jeb snapped, his tone bordering on hostile.

"Oh, no," I replied.

"Any kids?" his face took on an inquisitive look and he winked at me. "You know," he added.

I wasn't sure what he was asking me. Was he asking me if I liked girls? Or maybe he was asking because he actually was about to show me some antique porn or something? I wasn't sure where he was headed. "No. I don't have kids," I finally answered and he nodded his head.

"That's good. They can be a handful," the old cowboy said. He grew quiet for a moment as if he was contemplating something or maybe he was just remembering something about kids.

Jeb then stood up and walked over to an old Victorian style floor lamp at the opposite end of the sofa and turned it on. He handed me the viewer and said, "It works best the closer you are to the light, but not too close-the slides are kinda sensitive."

I slid down the sofa to where I could easily train the viewer on the light and held it up.

"Be sure you focus it. Just slide the tray back and forth until you find the image is nice and clear," he instructed. "That slide is my wife's favorite. It brings back bittersweet memories for her. She says it reminds her of our son. He died in the Gulf War years ago."

"I'm sorry to hear that."

I adjusted the viewer and the image slowly came into crisp focus. It was a real nice picture for the age of the optics, nothing to write home about. I was about to say something like, "Nice" and hand the viewer back to Jeb when something extraordinary happened.

The image moved!

I blinked my eyes and took the viewer from my face, and looked at the slide from over the top of the view port. I then placed the viewer back to my eyes and watched as the scene depicted on the slide came to life.

The viewpoint of the slide was changing as if it were a scene from a movie where the camera pans around a room.

It showed a library of books, a Nobel Prize residing in a small alcove-and a sullen old man brooding over a drink...

A HISTORY LESSON

John Wilcox was a world-renowned physicist, scientist, and a Nobel Laureate. And although he had solved the riddle of time, he was a very despondent man.

"John. John? JOHN!" The sound of her voice snapped Wilcox back to reality. "John? Are you listening to anything I'm saying?"

Wilcox glanced up from his glass to the concerned face of Susan Litchfield, a friend and colleague at the Institute.

"I've got to go. I have a board meeting in the morning," she stated, touching his arm tenderly. "Besides John, the answer to what ails you is not in that glass".

Wilcox stared at his colleague and muttered, "No. Not in here, Susan. In time," he sighed in a near whisper, jabbing his finger back and forth for some reason that escaped her.

Litchfield stared at him for a second, plopped down her glass of wine and launched herself out of her chair. "I'll see my way out."

As she passed Wilcox on her way to the door, she patted him on the shoulder as a sign of affection, and he nodded his head in response.

At the door, she paused and looked at the Nobel Prize displayed atop a pedestal that was tucked in the corner of the room. It had been there for over a decade. It was both a symbol of his great achievement and of his failure to replicate that achievement in even a small way. Her eyes filled with tears as she thought about the man Wilcox seemed to have become and she whispered softly to herself, "Where is the man who earned this?"

After a moment, she mustered the courage to turn to Wilcox and ask, "What happened to that man, John? What happened to that scientist who could see into the universe, who could probe the meaning of time and could unlock its secrets?"

Wilcox raised his head and looked up at Litchfield, shaking his head. "That man has no meaning. That man sees no future. That man is alone." He dropped his eyes to the floor and in a low voice said, "That man has no son." And tears began to well up in his eyes.

"John, it's 1970. Jerry died twenty years ago." She tried to sound sympathetic. "You have to let him go or it will destroy you. You have to go on with your life. You cannot change the past. You can't change history."

Wilcox suddenly became animated. "Can't change history, you say?" He slapped down his drink and slid partway out of his chair to a near standing position. "Are you so certain?" He seemed suddenly sure of himself, as if he knew something she didn't.

Litchfield looked puzzled. "What are you saying?"

As if flipping a switch, Wilcox reverted to the melancholy man he had been just moments before. "It's nothing. It's late and I've had too much to drink. Of course we can't change the past." He stood up all the way and walked over to Susan and took her hand. "I'm sorry. I've been a bad host tonight. I'll see you out."

He added, "And, Susan…?"

"Yes?"

"Thanks for coming over. Thank you for being a good friend. Thank you for being so tolerant of this foolish man."

"Sure, John. Anytime."

They hugged good night and Wilcox returned to his study.

He sat down behind his desk, opened the bottom drawer of the file cabinet next to him and pulled out a large brown leather portfolio. It was his scrapbook, and it contained the clippings of his life achievements and the reminders of his personal obsession with time.

He slowly turned the pages and spent a minute or two reflecting on each one. Each page contained a newspaper clipping or some kudo he had earned up to and including his crowning achievement-the Nobel Prize for Physics.

It was all there.

A perfect commentary on a perfect life. His graduation photo from MIT at the age of thirteen. His selection as Graduate Fellow at the Stanford Physics Department two years later. The three years he spent as head researcher at Fermi Labs and his cover picture on Time Magazine when he won the Nobel Prize for his contributions to the study of time.

But the pages didn't end there.

As he turned the last few of the scrapbook, near the end was a headline in the Ft. Worth Star-Telegram about an auto accident.

It was dated July 22, 1950 and read 'HIT AND RUN KILLS YOUNG BOY'. On the facing page, another read 'DRUNK DRIVER FOUND GUILTY OF MANSLAUGHTER'. Below the article was a picture of his son.

Wilcox closed the scrapbook and laid it on the desk. Then placed his head in his hands and sobbed.

* * *

The next morning as Wilcox, his head throbbing, was about to get himself a large glass of water from the office pods water cooler, Litchfield walked in. He needed the water to wash down the three aspirin he'd found after rummaging around in his desk for the last ten minutes.

Litchfield crossed the communal area as he drew the glass of water from the cooler. She stood eyeing him, making him nervous until finally he turned and asked, "What?"

"Well, I see you survived the night. How do you do it?"

"Do what?" Wilcox calmly replied.

"Drink like a fish and not show any sign of a hangover the next day. That's what."

"It's all in the genes, Ms. Geneticist," Wilcox retorted as he deftly moved the aspirins he was ready to swallow from his hand to his pocket. "So how did your board meeting go?"

"Oh, you know. Status reports, then the usual pressure and nonsense about achieving results that are meant to inspire us." Her lips turned almost into a slight sneer. "Like the three patents they've filed because of my research just isn't enough?"

"Glad it wasn't me." John muttered drolly.

Litchfield looked directly at Wilcox. "And by the way, when will you be ready to show off your new baby?"

"Soon."

He took a big gulp of water.

"That's what you said last week and last month and, I believe, last year? Isn't the Board breathing down your neck?"

"The Board!" he almost shouted in an angry tone. "Bunch of pencil neck paper pushers," he snarled, clearly agitated by the inquiry.

"Now, now, John. They do pay our salaries. We must be nice to the old ditties."

Wilcox shrugged. He knew that they were among some of the top scientists in their field who worked at the Mogollon Institute. The Institute, located at the local university in Ft. Worth, was famous for its breakthrough discoveries in physics, chemistry, and biology. They knew that The Institute was almost fascist when it came to security and the protection of their intellectual property.

In fact, the Institute left little to chance.

Researchers were sequestered behind locked doors, gated fenced facilities and, in the case of the larger, more physical projects like Wilcox, they were housed in a secure, guarded facility. They had even gone as far as segmenting the development and application portions for each project.

Once a researcher had proven the viability of his or her project, they were quickly reassigned and other researchers from the Institute would verify the project and then a third group would take over and develop and exploit the discovery's various applications.

None of the scientists on campus liked the process required by the Institute, but in exchange, they were allowed to do pure well-funded research without any government bureaucrats peering over their shoulders or some college board of regents doling out the funding at a rate that only a miser could love.

Wilcox took a quick glance about the pod, then stepped closer to Litchfield and whispered, "Those old ditties don't know squat." He took a quick glance around the office, once more verifying they were alone, then asked, "Would you like to see something that will give all those old ditties heart attacks?"

Litchfield gave him a puzzled look. Then a grin crossed her face. "Why you old con artist. You're hiding something from the board aren't you?" and then with a shock of realization she blurted, "You've completed your project!"

Wilcox grinned, scratched the closely cropped beard on his face and stifled a nervous chuckle. He wiggled his finger and uttered softly, "Come with me."

His female colleague followed Wilcox down the hall and outside into the parking lot. They climbed into Wilcox's SUV and proceeded to take the campus access road from the public portion of the university to the Institute's separate research facility.

Taking a small side drive, they soon encountered an imposing heavy steel automated security gate. The sign on the gate read, "LEVEL 3 PERSONNEL ONLY. ALL OTHERS REPORT TO CAMPUS SECURITY. TRESPASSERS WILL BE PROSECUTED." Wilcox punched in his security code and waited for the gate to open.

"Are you sure they will let me in?" Litchfield asked.

"You're in good standing with the board aren't you?" he asked, already knowing the answer.

She nodded.

"Plus you're with me," he stated and gave her a crooked grin.

The entrance drive was a mile and a half of winding road that weaved its way through a heavy stand of trees, ensuring a high level of anonymity.

Upon rounding the last curve in the drive, Litchfield quipped, "I can see why they call it the bunker."

The facility was a plain, one-story concrete structure that appeared to be set back into a hill. It had no windows, though it did have a large glass entryway.

"Is this the first time you've been out here?" Wilcox queried, the subject never really having come up before.

"My first time. We geneticists aren't known for causing things to explode or vaporize like some of our fellow researchers, so we're forced to work in the office pod."

"Trust me. You'll love it down there."

Litchfield thought to herself, *'Down there'?*

As they stepped up to the door, Wilcox turned to her and said in a very conspiratorial tone, "What I am about to show you is highly classified. I don't have to tell you what that means, do I?"

She nodded her head.

Stepping through the door, they immediately took ten steps down to a set of sliding glass doors that appropriately slid aside as they approached. Beyond them was a large well-lit lobby. In the center of the space was a large marble faced desk-and nothing else. No chairs or benches or fake potted plants.

Behind the desk was an older gentleman armed with an automatic pistol. The elderly man stood and stepped around his desk, blocking their path to the elevators. He approached the two scientists.

"Good morning, Dr. Wilcox," the guard said pleasantly as he ran a metal wand around the two visitors.

Wilcox took it in stride, replying with a smile, "Hi, Sam. How are you today?"

"Just great, Doctor," the guard stated as he finished wanding the two of them.

"I bet you're counting the days," Wilcox commented, making small talk.

"You know it, Doctor. I've just three weeks, four days and six hours to go. Then I'll be officially a reee-tired senior citizen. How about you doctor? When you going to give up this rat race?"

"Not for a while, Sam. I have too many things yet to do."

"Who's this young lady?"

"This is Dr. Susan Litchfield. She's with the Genetics Department.

"It's nice to meet you, Sam." Litchfield stated and then gushed, "This is the first time I've been here and I've worked at the Institute for more than ten years. It looks to be quite a place. I can't wait to see the rest of it."

"I call it home," Sam chuckled as he set the wand down.

"So what does that do?" she asked.

"It checks for recording devices and metal as in guns or knives," Sam explained.

"Oh" Susan uttered as she thought about what that could mean.

"Dr. Litchfield and I are going to the lab. I personally cleared her for this visit, okay?" Wilcox stated in a conspiratorial manner.

Sam gave him a sideways glance and said, "Ah…Sure, Doctor, I just need to verify her I.D." Sam stepped back behind the desk to his security console as Susan handed him her badge.

He scanned it and a green light illuminated on his console. Sam smiled and stated, "You're all clear. You can go now."

"Thanks Sam," Wilcox said as he guided his partner towards the elevators.

Sam waited until their backs were turned before pressing the button under the edge of his desk, unlocking the elevators.

Stepping on board the elevator, Wilcox swiped his card yet again and then pressed the button that read SUBLEVEL B. The doors closed and the elevator started a high-speed descent.

As they descended, Wilcox asked, "What do you know about time?"

"How far underground is Sublevel B?" she asked in reply.

"About two hundred feet. It will only take a few seconds to get there. These are high-speed elevators." He cleared his throat. "Now what do you know about time?" he pressed.

Susan creased her brow, raised her hand to her chin, arched an eyebrow and replied, "Hmm, Let's see. You can save it, spend it, waste it, lose it and theoretically fold it, is that right?" She added as an afterthought, "I tend to lose it in the morning mostly."

"Lose it?" he asked. "In the morning?"

"Well, yeah. It's not easy for a woman to get herself presentable every morning. All men have to do is brush their teeth, shave, comb their hair and put on some clothes."

"I wasn't aware you went in for all that foo foo stuff. I just thought you were naturally beautiful. A naturally beautiful, liberated woman, to be more precise." Wilcox turned his head to try and hide his smirk.

"I am, with the accent on woman. Better lose that smirk or you're liable to find out what a liberated woman can do to a chauvinist pig," she teased.

"Okay. Okay. But seriously, about time?" Wilcox pressed again.

She took a deep breath, exhaled and said, "Well, I remember Einstein said that space and time are connected in some way. And that your work revolved around his concept of time being another dimension of space."

"Good." Wilcox stated as the elevator doors opened. "Now let's take that a step further. A few hundred steps further." They stepped out of the elevator, and Wilcox quickly led the way down the hallway, around the corner and into his lab.

The laboratory made Litchfield gasp. It was enormous. It seemed to engulf them. The ceilings were at least fifty feet high and the room had to be a hundred feet long. Transformers lined the wall on the left and on the right, the wall was covered with computer towers and terminals. In the center of the room was a large control panel that faced a slightly raised platform that held a large silver cube. The Cube was maybe five feet by five feet.

At the far end of the cavernous room were several large tanks, similar to the fuel tanks you might see on a farm. They were raised about five feet off the ground and each held five hundred gallons. They were connected to each other on the platform and on their sides. In large yellow letters were painted the words 'NITROGEN'.

"Let's have a seat for a moment," he suggested.

The female scientist pulled a chair over and sat beside him as he reached into his desk drawer and pulled out a pad of paper. "I'm going to give you a crash course in the meaning of time."

"Please keep it in layman's terms," she said, giving him a look while still managing to smile at him.

"I'll keep it as simple as I can," he stated as he ripped a sheet of paper off the notepad and laid it in front of her. "What do you see?"

"I see a blank piece of paper."

"No, what you see is a representation of a two-dimensional space. It has length and width, but no depth. If you were a two dimensional creature, this is the type of 'world' you would inhabit."

She nodded affirmatively.

Wilcox then picked up a pencil and said rhetorically, "Now, let's see what a one dimensional world would look like." He then drew a straight line on the sheet of paper and said, "It would look like this-length, but without width or depth. Agreed?"

"It's hardly rocket science," she retorted curtly. "I think we can skip a few steps."

"I know this is quite basic, but bear with me," He cleared his throat before continuing. "Now, time to the two dimensional creature is a progression of his two-dimensional space above and below his plane. As his plane moves through time, in reality, it is moving through the 'space' around it." He moved the sheet of paper up and down above the desk.

"And to the one dimensional creature," he pointed to the pencil line he drew on the paper, "the progression of his one dimensional space, left or right of the line, gives him the impression of moving through time. In reality, he is really moving into the 'space' beside him." He then drew a series of parallel lines on the sheet of paper.

"Then you're saying, time to one is really space to another?" she sought to clarify.

"Correct! Time is only another dimension of space!" he proclaimed as if he were hosting a game show.

"So what about us three-dimensional creatures," she asked. "Is our dimension of time"

"Just another dimension of space." Wilcox interjected, cutting off her comment.

"Would that be the same for the fourth, fifth, sixth and further dimensional realities too?" she asked.

"Yes. The time dimension of the fourth dimensional creature would be a space dimension of a fifth dimensional creature. The same for the fifth dimensional world and the sixth. Each successive time dimension is really a space dimension for the level of reality around it."

Litchfield was quiet for a moment while she thought things through and finally asked, "What does this have to do with your project?"

Wilcox smiled and said in a low whisper, "I've created a way to enter that fourth dimension of space."

Litchfield remained silent for several seconds, giving him a very skeptical look. "How?" she finally uttered.

"I'll show you. Just sit there for a few moments. I'll be right back," he said, hurrying out of the lab.

Litchfield started to get up to explore her surroundings, but thought better of it. Just as she sat back down, she heard and felt a deep vibrating hum. Soon after that, Wilcox came back to the lab, locking the laboratory doors behind him.

"I've fired up the generators. Just sit tight."

Wilcox then moved to the control panel on the sidewall. He pressed a few buttons, turned a few dials, and the transformers came to life. The sound they generated at first was near deafening, but soon dropped several tens of decibels, leaving just a strong background hum.

Wilcox then looked at Litchfield and beckoned her to join him on the platform.

Cautiously, she followed him up next to the silver Cube. The sound of nitrogen gas flowing in the pipes above and below the platform added to the steady drone of the transformers, making it difficult to keep her focus.

Wilcox stood grinning at her as he stepped to the side of the Cube, pressed a large lever down, and then stood back.

Litchfield stood transfixed as she stared at the Cube, really a block with adjustable top and sides.

As she stared at it, it suddenly transformed. Whereas she had been looking straight at the Cube, watching her reflection in its mirror-like finish, she could now see right through it to the lab wall on the other side of it. The sides and top expanded and opened up a five foot by five foot space. Her eyes grew wide and she started to say something, but Wilcox beat her to it.

"Isn't it cool? The space can open up once the systems are up and at full capacity. I'd explain how, but I'm afraid it would take days and we haven't the time now. We need to keep moving."

Inside the space of the tower, on the floor, was a grid.

"Now. Pick up that rubber ball over there," he instructed.

Litchfield picked up the ball that sat on a small table next to the tower and handed it to Wilcox.

"No. No," he admonished. "Place it in the center of the grid inside the tower."

She gave him an odd look, began to place the ball inside the tower-then quickly withdrew it. "It's ice cold in there!"

"You women! What happened to that extra layer of fat you're suppose to have?"

"Don't get smart, buster," she growled, then asked, "Is it safe?"

"It's just cold air. Go ahead. Put the ball in."

Litchfield slowly extended her arm into the space within the tower and deposited the ball on the grid. The cold made her hand and arm tingle. "My skin feels like it's crawling."

"That's normal. Now, pull your hand out."

She quickly retracted her arm and asked, "Now what?"

"Look back inside the Cube and tell me what you see."

She shrugged and turned back towards the Cube and peered inside. The ball was gone. All she could see was the opposite wall of the lab.

"It's *gone*! Where did it go?"

"Not where – when!"

Litchfield looked confused. "What do you mean?"

Wilcox smiled. "It's there, but not for us. At least not for us here."

"You're talking double-talk," she said, getting annoyed.

"Not really," he replied. "If you were there and not here, you could see it."

Litchfield got angry. "Quit fooling with me Wilcox. Explain what happened."

"Stick your head in the tower."

"What?!"

"I said, stick your head in the tower."

Litchfield didn't think Wilcox would let harm come to her, yet this seemed like a crazy thing to do. Sheepishly she asked, "Why?"

"Just put your head in the tower and tell me what you see," he said firmly.

Susan hesitated a few beats, then slowly, inch by inch she leaned into the tower.

The cold wrapped itself around her head as if it were a down pillow. Her face tingled and the tip of her nose began to feel as if someone was sticking it with needles. The chill of the air sent shivers down her spine.

She was about to pull back when she opened her eyes and looked down under her chin. The rubber ball was right there. A quick glance up and she realized that she was unable to see the wall of the lab out the other side of the cube. The space she was in was enveloped in a gray haze.

"Oh my Lord!" she exclaimed then felt a wave of sudden dizziness wash over her. She quickly pulled out of the tower then looked back. The ball was gone and she could once more look through the cube and see the other wall of the lab.

"John, I'm light headed and feel like I'm going to pass out."

"That's normal. It'll pass fairly quickly"

Litchfield straightened up and then inquired, "I don't understand. Why can I see the ball when I'm inside the tower but not when I'm outside?"

"Because when you're outside the tower you are in your own space dimension. But inside the tower you are in the same space dimension as the ball. The fourth dimension."

Her eyebrows lifted as she blurted out. "Jesus, John, you let me stick my head in another dimension." She looked long and hard at the man she thought was her friend.

"Yes, that's right. And by moving around inside the fourth dimension you are actually moving through time."

"So I just time traveled?"

Wilcox nodded.

"That's Incredible!" she shrieked with excitement.

Wilcox just stood there grinning at her.

Finally, beaming a huge smile across her face,
Litchfield looked him in the eye and asked, "Why haven't you told the board about this? They will totally flip out!"

"It's not ready yet," he said evasively.

"What? Not Ready? But it works, John! It works!"

"I still haven't completed the work on the time control mechanism," he stated, half truthfully. He looked at Litchfield and pleaded, "Susan, please keep this to yourself. I would really appreciate that."

"Sure, John. Sure. But I don't understand…"

"I have my reasons. Please?"

"OK. Mums the word."

* * *

"Dr. Wilcox!" someone bellowed from behind him as he was leaving his office en route to the bunker. He turned and saw it was George Avondale, Chairman of the Board for the Mogollon Institute.

"I need to speak with you, Dr. Wilcox. Please come with me to my office," Avondale stated curtly.

32

Whenever Wilcox met with Avondale, it made him feel as though he were a child in school, caught misbehaving and on the way to the Principal's office for punishment.

Avondale set a brisk pace as he seemed to be racing Wilcox back to his office – an office paneled with rich dark oak and featuring two full walls of built-in bookshelves filled with books in mint condition. Wilcox doubted anyone had ever read them, least of all Avondale.

The Chairman pointed to the overstuffed seat in front of his desk. As he moved around behind it, he said, "Please sit, Dr. Wilcox."

Wilcox accepted the invitation and sat down as Avondale circled around to his imposing dark polished and carved desk. The professor waited for Avondale to begin.

Once Avondale had settled into his big executive office chair, he pulled a large gray folder from a drawer and opened it to a page that was titled, Current Project. Avondale made a show of acting as though he needed to refresh his memory in regards to the project. Actually, this was Avondale's of trying to intimidate the scientists because he felt threatened by their intellects.

Wilcox wondered why he hadn't been forced to endure one of Avondale's infamous talks prior to this moment. It was out of character for the Chairman to accept the written reports and not follow up with an interview every ninety days.

When he had finished reviewing the file Avondale grunted and looked down his glasses at Wilcox. "Doctor, the Board has asked me to speak with you about your research project. It's been…" he thumbed a page in the folder, "six years now and we've seen no real progress."

"I'm close, Mr. Avondale."

Closer than you think.

"As you know, Doctor, the Institute allows a great deal of leeway in regards to the length of time it takes our researchers to develop and test their experiments. We generously provide funding with little in the way of accounting for its use. But your project has consumed a large portion of the budget and space within the facilities labs without there being any appearance of financial benefit to the Institute for the foreseeable future."

"Yes, I understand, but…"

Avondale cut him off with a sharp wave of his hand.

"Dr. Wilcox," Avondale said abruptly. "Let me finish. I'm sorry to be the bearer of bad news," though his face looked decidedly cheerful. He continued, "But there are other projects that show more potential in regards to succeeding in providing the financial return needed to operate the Institute."

"But, Mr. Avondale…"

The Chairman cut him off yet again.

"Dr. Wilcox," Avondale stated in a firm, cold voice, sounding to Wilcox as if he were addressing a failing student. "Despite the time, money and resources that the Institute has expended on your projects behalf, it doesn't appear as though we can expect a positive outcome anytime soon. With what we have committed to your fruitless project we could fund at least five others that are far more promising financially."

"Mr. Avondale, I am so close," Wilcox repeated. "If you would only give me a few more…"

Avondale waved his hand abruptly cutting off John yet again. "I'm sorry Doctor."

His tone had an air of finality to it.

"The Board has decided to terminate your project as of tomorrow. Of course, you can submit a new project for approval, if you wish. Or we can assign you to another project where you can assist the team and thus keep your position with the Institute. Either way we will need a commitment from you within two weeks. I expect that you'll leave the lab as it is and turn over all of your notes, in case the review board can see an opportunity for the Institute to, perhaps, recoup some of our losses on this project."

"Of course," Wilcox mumbled. He was in shock that Avondale had actually threatened his position with the Institute. He stood to shake Avondale's hand but Avondale made no effort to meet Wilcox half way and thus dismissed him.

As Wilcox turned to leave, Avondale admonished him one more time. "You're a valuable asset to the Institute, Dr. Wilcox and you should be spending your time and ours on a project that will generate better results for both of us."

The man was heartless and Wilcox knew it would be of no use arguing. Avondale was strictly a numbers man. If a project didn't add up to profit, he quickly and permanently closed it down. Unless he told him what was really happening with the project, he knew it was to be terminated tomorrow at the end of the day.

As Wilcox stepped into the hallway outside the office,
he thought to himself.

Tomorrow, his project in Time would be history, but there was still tonight.

Tonight-he would make up for the past.

* * *

Upon leaving Avondale's office, he decided to go directly to the bunker. He chose not to take his vehicle so as not to draw any undue attention.

He walked through the security gate and then cut across the hills on a well-worn footpath that cut over a mile off rather than following the road. As he hiked through the woods, the wind grew chilly and the sound rustling through the trees reminded him of a somber march.

Arriving at the bunker, he slid his card through the reader and entered. The lobby, unlike earlier, was now dimly lit by a few recessed ceiling spotlights directed into the corners of the large room. Sam, the security guard, was surprised to see him.

"Dr. Wilcox. What are you doing here this time of night?"

"I have few things to tidy up, Sam."

"Um, well, you know that employees are not allowed in here after hours? Rules, you know," he said, picking up his logbook.

"I know the rules, Sam. I'll only be a minute."

"I really shouldn't."

"Look. If someone finds out," Wilcox smiled, "tell them I tied you up."

"Very funny," Sam replied.

"Do it for old time's sake," Wilcox said affectionately. Almost a farewell.

Sam looked at him in a funny way, then made his decision. "Well, alright. Just this once." He put his logbook down and tossed it on his desk.

Wilcox thanked him and proceeded to the lab.

Before he entered, he turned on the generators in the service room and checked to see their voltage output. The output had to be at a perfect level for tonight.

Satisfied, he entered the lab.

He moved to the control panel and checked the displays of dials and other indicators. They all were showing optimum levels.

There was just one more task to perform.

He hastened over to the five by five-foot silver cube as the sound of the cold nitrogen pulsed through the pipes above his head and snaked its way into a conductor coupling at the top of the cube.

At the foot of the cube, he pulled the lever that he had shown Litchfield, but this time, when he pulled it back, he also pushed it sideways, like putting a car into third gear.

Immediately, the Cube began to enlarge.

The top and sides of the Cube began to move out, making the small opening in the tower grow larger and larger. In tandem, the low vibration coming from the room began to growl louder and louder until the steel supports visible in the ceiling above began to shake and shudder.

Wilcox moved quickly to the control panel, turned a few dials, and the vibrations settled down to a low hum. He wiped the anxious sweat from his brow and returned to the tower.

The tower now had an eight-foot tall and five foot wide opening.

Wilcox knew that the next part was going to be tricky.

His objective was Ft. Worth. That was easy. That's where the Institute resided. The trick was the time.

He hadn't had the chance to perfect the actual calibration of the targeting of time and, since the Board was closing him down, he never would. It was risky, but no risk was too great for a loving father.

With time literally running out from more than one perspective, he had to make his best calculation and hope for the best. It was huge risk, one in which he was betting his life.

With the clock ticking, he pulled a small hand-held calculator from a drawer in the control panel. He quickly synchronized the settings required to connect with the exact place in time he desired.

It was complicated, much like calculating the trajectory of a missile meant to intercept another missile without knowing from which direction the first missile was coming. He was sure to include the variables of Chaos Theory and for the shifting of the solar alignments until finally he accepted he had reached the correct solution to the problem.

He walked back to the control panel and entered the numbers into its keypad. Wilcox waited until the display above the keypad read 'COORDINATES ENTERED. TARGET TIME CONFIRMED. ACCESS CYCLE 24 HOURS.'

Wilcox turned and walked up to the Cube's opening. He took a deep breath and stepped inside.

He felt a rush of cold air and his skin felt as if something was crawling underneath it. He then felt a wave of dizziness sweep over him and the space began swirling around him.

Then he blacked out.

* * *

John Wilcox opened his eyes and realized he was flat on his back, gazing up at a crisp, clear night sky populated with thousands of bright stars.

He slowly stood up and oriented himself to his new surroundings. He was outside in the woods. The terrain was that of rolling hills just like those that surrounded the Institute.

It made perfect sense, he realized. He was standing in the exact spot the Institute's bunker would occupy twenty years from now.

Glancing around he saw a sign, the kind used when a major building project was planned for a site. This one stated: 'FUTURE SITE OF THE MOGOLLON INSTITUTE'. He would use that sign to locate exactly where the portal would reappear for his return trip home in twenty-four hours.

Satisfied that he had managed to get the location correct, he now needed to know the date and the time. The area wasn't nearly as populated as it would be in the future, but he knew there was a Greyhound bus station less than a mile down the road. He used to ride the bus, back and forth, from school to his home in San Antonio, when he was a student at the university.

An hour or so later, Wilcox entered the bus terminal. He quickly scanned the waiting area and looked for the wall clock.

It read 6:45 PM.

He knew the time.

But what was the date?

He hurried over to the newsstand and looked at the newspapers stacked on the floor. He read the date on that day's Ft. Worth Star-Telegram.

July 22nd, 1950.

The day his son was killed.

He not only knew the date, but the time of his son's death. The investigation recorded the time of the hit and run at 7:28.

Thank God his calculations were correct.

But he had less than 45 minutes to reach his son and stop him from entering the intersection. He ran the numbers over in his mind. The scene of the accident was only a mile away. He could be there in time, especially if he cut across the park.

He jogged off towards downtown and shortly found himself in the park across from where his son was brutally run down. All he had to do was pass the picnic area, go down and around the small lake, then up over the rise bordering the main drive through town. There, he would be in a position to stop his son before he entered the intersection.

Despite there being a number of light posts in the park, it was a cool night and a wispy fog had settled in over the area surrounding the lake. It made it difficult to see things more than a few yards in the distance.

As he approached the small lake, he could just make out a young boy perched at the edge of the water. He was waving his arms frantically and yelling as loud as he could for help.

Despite being pressed for time, Wilcox jogged up to the boy, who appeared to be twelve or thirteen, and asked him what was wrong. The boy was in near hysterics, making it hard to understand him.

"Please Mister, help me," the boy cried out frantically.

Wilcox eyed the boy who kept turning to look at the lake in between pleadings.

"I'm sorry I haven't the time. I can't help you, son. I have to be someplace very important," Wilcox yelled as he tried to keep moving.

"It's not me sir, it's my brother!" the young boy shouted as he pointed anxiously towards the lake. "He's drowning," he cried out.

Wilcox peered into the fog-shrouded darkness and noticed that the surface of the lake was disturbed about forty feet from shore. He rubbed his eyes, hoping for a clearer view. When he looked again, he saw a small body thrashing about in the water.

Wilcox was now in a quandary. If he helped this boy, he might miss helping his own son. He had to leave. There wasn't time for both.

He looked once more at the small boy thrashing in the water and then off into the distance towards the intersection.

"Mister please, I can't swim. I can't help him. Please save him Mister, please," the boy begged as the thrashing in the water ceased.

"Oh my God, he's dying," the young boy cried. "He's gone, my brother is gone," the boy bellowed and then began to sob pathetically.

Reluctantly, Wilcox kicked off his shoes and jumped off the bank.

He couldn't let the boy drown.

He swam out to the last spot he'd seen the boy but couldn't see anything now, not even a ripple was left. Then suddenly a small hand broke the surface a few feet to his right, and he grabbed it.

Wilcox managed to pull the almost lifeless body to shore where he quickly began trying to resuscitate the boy.

The small quiet body didn't respond at first, but after a few minutes of chest compressions, the boy began spitting up water.

Wilcox quickly turned him on his side and then, when he'd stop spitting water, he rolled him back over and began to give the boy mouth to mouth.

Wilcox lost track of time as he fought to save the boy. After several exchanges of breath, the boy came back to life and vomited even more water.

"You're okay, son. You're going to be all right. Just lie here a few minutes and let yourself relax and recover a bit."

The boy rolled towards Wilcox and clung to him for all he was worth. His brother soon joined in the hug fest, now crying tears of joy. Wilcox, for the first time in years, felt good about himself.

"It's okay. You're going to be just fine." Wilcox nurtured the two boys for a moment, and then he realized he didn't have time for this.

He had to save his own son.

"I'm sorry but I have to go," Wilcox stated as he extricated himself from their embrace.

Turning to run towards the intersection, Wilcox heard the older boy yell, "Thank You, Mister, Thank you".

Wilcox couldn't respond. He was too focused on fulfilling his goal of saving his son. He ran as fast as he could for the top of the rise and as he topped the crest, he could see that he was already too late.

In rapid succession, but as if in slow motion, he saw his son on his bike approach the intersection. To the boy's right sped a small pickup. It was headed directly for him.

Then the inevitable happened.

Wilcox screamed but no one heard him. "Jerry, STOP! *STOP!*"

Wilcox watched in horror as the pickup slammed into his son's bike sending his broken body 30 feet across the intersection and into the park.

"No! No!" Wilcox cried. "Oh please, God, no."

Wilcox fell to the ground, kneeled in the wet grass and, bowing his head, sobbed into his hands.

* * *

Defeated and despondent, Wilcox trudged back to the bus station. He found a seat away from the other travelers and sat pondering what to do with his future.

He was an old fool. He'd stupidly believed that he could play God and change history.

Soon he found the bus station had emptied out except for a mother and her young son. He watched them as the minutes ticked by, envious of her and her son, for he'd lost his son a second time.

Glancing at the station's clock, he realized he was stuck here, killing time for the next twenty odd hours, before he could return through the portal to his own time.

Oh God, what he'd give to have just a few of the precious minutes of that time back, prior to his failed attempt to rescue his son, but it was not to be. He had plenty of time now, now that he didn't need it, now that it wasn't where or when he had needed it!

He silently cursed himself and the fates.

The thoughts of time spun in ever-widening circles in his mind and he thought he would go stark raving mad, but somehow he clung to his composure and tried to think of something else, anything else.

He needed something positive and his mind wandered back to the small boy he'd saved from the lake. He wondered what would become of him. Then he realized he didn't even know the boy's name and admonished himself for having overlooked that small detail.

As he sat there contemplating the boy's future, he began absently fingering a small piece of paper he found in his pocket. He thought it was odd he found it because he didn't remember having placed it there. He pulled the piece of paper out of his pocket and unfolded it to reveal an address. It was handwritten in block letters, much like those of a child just learning to write or in a hurry.

Was it the boy's address?

He remembered the city layout and realized the address was only a few short blocks away.

He walked the distance at a leisurely pace, for time was his to waste tonight. But despite his lethargic stroll, it only took ten minutes to find the home.

The house was small and rundown, with two bikes in the front yard neatly parked among the wilted shrubbery. He hesitated for a moment and then decided it wouldn't hurt to ask. That way he could look up the boy in the future. So he walked up to the door and knocked several times before a young woman answered the door.

"Yes, can I help you?" she asked suspiciously.

"Um, yes, hello," Wilcox then hesitated a moment before he continued, "I'm the man who saved the young boy earlier."

"Oh my Lord, Please come in," she offered abruptly, much more open and friendly.

"Oh no, I couldn't, I was stopping by to find out how he's doing."

"His older brother told me all about what you did. We are in your debt, sir."

"Oh, please, I'm just glad I was able to save him. Really it was nothing." Wilcox lied through his teeth. It had cost him everything.

"Are you sure you wouldn't like to come in and have a seat, maybe something to drink?" she offered again.

"No. No, I'm sure. I have a bus to catch but thank you. I really just wanted to check and be sure he was okay."

"Oh he's fine. He's running around here somewhere with his big brother," she stated as she looked back into the house for the boy.

"Well, I'd tell the boy to stay away from the water until he learns to swim," Wilcox suggested.

"You can be sure I will and I'll be sure to include you in my prayers," she stated.

Wilcox nodded humbly and turned to leave, only to stop and ask, "May I ask your name?"

"It's Marguerite. I'm his mother."

"And the boy's name?"

"It's Lee. Lee Harvey Oswald."

I sat stunned for a few minutes, trying to understand what I had just seen.

It didn't make any sense. How could a simple stereopticon show me what had to have been a movie? I even heard the words as the actors interacted on the screen. I turned the viewer over and around several times and I was convinced it was made of a few small pieces of wood, a couple of glass lenses and nothing else. It had no power source and the only moveable part was the slide holder that went back and forth an inch or two in order to allow people to focus it, based on their vision.

Jeb, grinning widely, asked, "So, what do you think?"

"Well, I a...I don't know what to think. How does it work?"

"I haven't a clue, but sure is interesting, ain't it?" Jeb replied.

"Where did you get it?" I asked, as I flipped the viewer over and checked for the battery compartment. There wasn't one. I surmised as such.

The old man smiled. I swore his eyes smiled, too.

"We found the box of slides many years ago. My wife and I have differing opinions on what they are."

"What do you think?" I asked.

"My wife, she thinks it works by magic. She says the slides are magical because they portray events in alternative realities. She's like that. Into paranormal stuff like that." He then leaned forward in his chair again and in a low voice he whispered, "Me, I think the slides are from another planet."

"Another planet, huh." I replied absently as I continued to check out the viewer. Jeb must have thought I was making fun of him because he became defensive right away.

"What? You think that sounds crazy or something? If you're so smart, what do you think they are?" Jeb groused at me.

"Oh, no, that wasn't what I meant. I was just repeating what you said as I thought about it. That's all. I really don't have any idea what it is or how it works. But I've got to tell you, it's incredible."

Jeb, that old cowboy, shrugged and sat back into his recliner where, by the look on his face, I assumed he was thinking hard about something. As he sat there contemplating whatever it was, he absently reached into his pocket and pulled out a small bag of tobacco and a package of rolling papers. As he continued sitting there, thinking, he rubbed the pouch with his fingers as if he was trying to crush whatever was inside.

Then suddenly he looked off towards the kitchen and slowly tucked the tobacco pouch and papers back into his shirt pocket. Apparently he was not supposed to be smoking.

Puzzled, I lowered the stereopticon to my lap and pondered what I had just seen. How could a simple, flat celluloid slide transform into a three-dimensional movie? It didn't make sense. It was almost as if it actually was magic.

"I hope you like guacamole because it's one of our favorites," Helen stated as she entered the room and set down a large bowl of corn chips and two bowls of dipping sauce. As she did so, she glanced at Jeb, who quickly looked away, avoiding eye contact with her.

"It's homemade and it's the hit of the State Fair every year," Jeb added as he pretended to be busy looking for another slide to view.

"He's just partial to the cook is all," Helen retorted modestly. Then she grabbed a big corn chip, scooped out a glob of guacamole and handed it to me saying, "Try it, you'll like it."

I did, and it was delicious. "Great," I mumbled with my mouthful, as I savored the flavor.

"Here. Try the chipotle, too." Helen insisted as she dipped a small corner of a big chip in the dip and handed it to me.

Not wanting to appear standoffish, I dipped the chip myself a second time, gathering a large glob of dip on it before I tossed it in my mouth saying, "I like chipotle." As I popped it into my mouth, Jeb spoke up.

"I'd be careful with that one. It has a bit of a bite to it." Jeb grinned, knowing it was too late.

As soon as I bit down, my mouth practically burst into flames. Her chipotle sauce was the hottest sauce I'd ever eaten-well at least tried to eat. Instantly I coughed up the chip and chipotle dip, crying out in anguish in the process, while launching part of the chip into the bowl of dip itself three feet away.

Tears immediately began streaming down my cheeks and I struggled to catch my breath, sucking copious amounts of air in and out through my mouth in an effort to cool the burning sensation. It only made it worse.

"Oh dear," Helen remarked, "it was too much for him, I'm afraid."

Through my tear-filled eyes, I could see Jeb staring at me with disdain. Obviously, he liked the chipotle dip, and I had ruined it with my projectile slobbering. It was also clear he was getting quite the kick out of seeing me try to cope with the liquid fire that I had unwittingly imbibed.

"Jeb, be a good host and get the young man a beer to put that fire out." Helen tersely directed Jeb, who slowly stood up and asked, "Want a beer?"

I nodded furiously as I was suddenly overwhelmed by a coughing spell.

"Don't puke in my guacamole," Jeb shouted as he stepped towards the garage. When he reached the door, he stopped and stated. "I don't drink that imported crap. Can you live with a domestic?"

God, he was taking his good old sweet time, obviously enjoying my plight.

"Sure, whatever you got." I wheezed between gasps of air and then he disappeared into the garage. Somehow, Jeb had pegged me for the import beer drinker I was.

"I'm so sorry. I really should have warned you." Helen stated with empathy as she patted my hand. "Just eat several chips with guacamole, it'll help cut the burn," she shared in a motherly fashion as she stood up and left for the kitchen once again.

As I stuffed several chips caked with guacamole into my mouth, Jeb stepped back into the house, from the garage, carrying two cans of Coors beer.

He handed one of them to me and said, "You can't get these where you're from - can you?"

I nodded. He was right again. I found myself quickly becoming impressed with Jeb's powers of observation. He had to have picked up on my east coast accent and knew Coors was difficult to get east of the Mississippi.

Despite having lived in Los Angeles for nearly a dozen years, my New York accent with still there, if you listened.

Jeb listened.

I drained the Coors in a couple of large gulps and let out a satisfied sigh, having put the fire out with a combination of the chips, guacamole and beer.

Relieved at being able to breathe without pain once again, I blurted out what I frequently told people I met at parties in Los Angeles about my accent. 'You can take the boy out of Brooklyn, but you can't take Brooklyn out of the boy.'

Jeb sat looking at me for the longest time as if I had just said something in gibberish, then stated coolly, "I suppose that's true enough."

He glanced at me, picked up the small metal box from the table again and held it close to his chest, like some valuable antique. He gently removed another slide from the box. "Here, take a look at it and tell me what you think." Jeb demanded.

I switched the slides, handing back the first slide to Jeb, who promptly tucked it back into the box, then leaned back while still clutching the box and watched me intently.

I tilted it towards the light once again and there, as before, right before my eyes, the slide came to life.

The moving picture showed the inside of a ship's cabin. In the bunk against the far wall was a young Japanese girl. The waif was frightened, sobbing, and having a terrible nightmare…

THE ORACLE

Kami bolted upright and screamed. The dream had seemed so real, the soldiers so close. As she tried to scream again, her small body was racked by a fit of coughing, which shook her body as the terror of the nightmare had shaken her soul.

She was back on the island.

The soldiers were once again ordering the crowd of people to move deeper into the cave, despite the voice blaring over loudspeakers, begging them to surrender, promising they would be treated well.

"Ignore the man on the speakers," a sergeant yelled over the din. He was very tall for Japanese, with a thin jagged scar running down the side of his face. He screamed again, "He is our enemy. Do not be fooled. He will kill you and eat our children if you surrender." As he threatened, he and several other soldiers pushed the crowd of civilians further into the cave with the points of their bayonets.

Suddenly, there was a horrific explosion at the mouth of the cave, punctuated by the tell-tale rata-tat-tat of machine gun fire that the inhabitants believed was aimed at them. Their fear drove the now panicked crowd deeper into the dark cavern. Dirt and rocks began falling from the cave's ceiling, as bombs continued to explode outside the cave, causing the ground to tremble like a small earthquake.

The rain of rocks and dirt forced the crowd to hug the walls as a thick cloud of dust formed, blocking out their view of the cave's mouth and making breathing difficult. Flushed with fear, the crowd pressed in upon itself, forming a tight knot of humanity in the rear of the cave.

Suddenly a soldier, engulfed in flames, burst though the dust cloud, stumbled and collapsed onto the cave floor right at Kami's feet. The flames licked at them, threatening to set her on fire too.

She screamed yet again.

"Wake up, child, wake up!" a gentle voice summoned her from her nightmare. "It's alright. You're okay. I'm right here." The gentle voice continued to assure her that she was fine now. "It was only a dream, my sparrow."

Kami was afraid to open her eyes for fear she'd see the burning soldier at her feet. But the voice was so reassuring, so comforting, and so familiar.

"Please, my dear, open your eyes, you'll see it is safe. It was just a bad dream. Please, Kami. I'm here to protect you."

Kami began to slowly open her eyes, only to be racked by another coughing fit that seemed to last for the longest of time. It left her feeling as if she would suffocate from the lack of air.

A hand gently patted and then rubbed her back helping to ease the muscle spasms caused by the coughing fit. Kami, now fully awake, was still a bit unsure of where she was but snuggled into her aunt's arms, ever grateful for her comforting.

"There, there, my sparrow, her aunt Koshu comforted her. "Everything is all right. You are safe here. See, you are in our cabin, on the ship. Do you remember?"

Kami nodded as she took in the somewhat familiar surroundings. She looked around the cabin and saw her kimono hanging on the back of the cabin door. She saw her two young cousins asleep in the next bunk and she once more felt the comforting hum and vibration from the ship's engines. Slowly, it came back to her. They were on an ocean-going freighter.

She remembered the adults called the ship a steamer because it used steam to power its huge propeller. The familiar sights and sounds soothed her and the terror that had seemed so real, just moments before, faded into the recesses of her mind.

"There now, let's dry those tears. We can't have those beautiful green eyes of yours all blurry now, can we?" her aunt Koshu whispered as she wiped away the streaks of tears on Kami's face with her kimono's sleeve. "For the life of me child, I can't understand how you could have such lovely green eyes. You are Japanese, not Caucasian. Your mother and father must have had some white people stock in them."

The mention of her mother caused little Kami to instantly burst into tears all over again.

"Oh no, I'm so sorry, child," Koshu apologized. "I didn't mean to remind you of her. I know how terrible it must have been to see her die. I'm so sorry," she stated as she drew Kami close and rubbed her back to comfort her.

"I miss her so," Kami mumbled between her sobs.

"I know my child, I miss her too," Koshu replied, fighting back tears of her own. "We will soon be at my home," Aunt Koshu murmured, as she held ten-year-old Kami close and rocked her gently back and forth. "I will show you my garden and perhaps you can help me care for it. Would you like that?"

Kami nodded.

"Soon you will only remember the good times with your mother and you'll forget all about Okinawa," her aunt stated as she laid Kami back down upon the bunk. "A new day will be dawning soon bringing us one day closer to home. Now try to go back to sleep, okay?"

Kami nodded ever so slightly and quickly drifted back to sleep, even before her aunt had finished pulling the covers back up and tucked her in. Knowing she would not be able to sleep herself, she kissed Kami on the cheek, checked her two sons to be sure they were covered snugly, and then went out on deck to watch the sunrise.

The ship's young captain was standing at the rail smoking a cigarette. While he stared at the barely visible horizon in the predawn haze, Koshu appeared.

To Koshu, the man was far too young to be a captain and she was curious as to how he had become one so soon.

"Good morning, Captain," Koshu replied demurely.

"Is everything all right?" he asked.

"I'm sorry. Did Kami's crying wake you?" she asked in reply.

"No, I was already up. We are crossing a dangerous stretch of sea this morning and I like to be on the bridge, should we run into any trouble."

Keeping a respectful tone, she asked him to explain how he had managed to be given such an honor and responsibility at such a young age.

"My father and his father before him were captains of vessels just like this one. I was raised on this ship. From a young age, I was groomed to one day take my father's position, so when the navy conscripted him he left me in charge of the vessel and our family's wellbeing."

"The Imperial Navy did not want you as well?" Koshu asked.

"They deemed I was too valuable captaining this ship, so I was left to do that which I am best suited. I have done my father proud. I have completed many voyages between our homeland and Korea and the Philippines. I was on the return leg of a voyage that took me past Okinawa when I spotted your signal on the beach."

"I'd like to thank you again, for rescuing us," Koshu stated.

The young captain became pensive. "It is a shame that only the liars and fanatics are left to defend our homeland. I don't understand why they would not let the civilians on Okinawa surrender to the Americans. The war is lost but it seems the military is willing to take the entire nation down with them."

He paused a moment before continuing. "Their lies, I was told, made many of the poor civilians take their own lives rather than surrender to the Americans."

Koshu became sullen. "Kami's mother was one of them. The young child watched her jump."

The Captain grimaced. "It must have been hard for the young girl to have watched her mother choose death by jumping from the cliffs into the sea."

"Yes," Koshu replied. "She has nightmares about it. I hope she will be able to forget and move on, but it was so traumatic. Her mother was so frightened. There was nothing I could do to stop her. I was lucky to have saved Kami."

The Captain stood silently, shaking his head for a moment and then asked, "How were you able to escape the murderous soldiers?"

Koshu thought back over the last terrible days. "The cave we were in had a large pool of water at the rear of it," Koshu explained. "I could see a bright patch of light at the bottom along the edge of a large overhang. I swam down and discovered that the light was coming from an opening in the ceiling of a hidden chamber. So I swam back up and gathered up the children. Then together we swam for the light."

She grew quiet for a moment as she wiped away a few tears, then continued. "We were lucky. The hidden chamber was above the water and we were able to climb out on to the beach and into the sea cave. If it had been high tide, I doubt we could have escaped. We went several days without food or water as we waited for the fighting to end. During that time, Kami developed a bad cough and the boys both came down with colds. The cave was so damp and cold at night, but I dared not make a fire for fear we would be discovered."

She squeezed the young captain's arm. "We are very thankful you stopped for us, Captain."

"It is what any good man would do," he stated as he continued looking out to sea.

"How many more days until we reach port?" Koshu asked.

The captain turned and smiled at her saying, "We should be in Hiroshima in a week or so, provided the weather holds."

"That is wonderful news. I can't wait until we are home again, safe and sound," she stated as she bowed and returned to her cabin.

Koshu lay down in her bunk and quickly dozed off. But less than an hour later, there was a very loud booming thud, and the ship shook so violently that Koshu and the children were thrown from their bunks onto the floor.

The children immediately began to cry and Koshu, not knowing exactly what was wrong, knew they needed to get dressed and get out on deck.

Just as she managed to get the boys dressed, the cabin door flung open and the First Mate charged in with his hands full of life preservers. "Here, put these on quickly. Then follow me," he ordered. With Koshu still struggling to get the boys' vest straps tied, the First Mate marched off with Koshu and the children staggering after him.

"What's happening?" Kami asked as they stumbled down the deck that was now tilted to port twenty degrees.

"Oh God, I think we've been hit by a torpedo and we're sinking." Koshu cried.

Kami and the boys now clung to her tightly, slowing their progress to the point that they were almost standing still.

The First Mate raced back for his charges, scooping up the two boys and ordering Koshu to bring the girl. He led them to a lifeboat that was partly lowered and placed the boys inside before helping Koshu and Kami climb in. He then ordered the two deckhands, standing next to the boat, to finish lowering the boat.

Once on the water, the two deck hands slid down ropes to the boat, where they took up oars and frantically rowed with all of their strength to escape the ship's suction vortex as it sank.

From less than a hundred yards away, Koshu, the children and the three crewmen watched, in stunned horror, as the ship rolled over on its side, then broke in half at the huge hole where the torpedo had struck.

There was a momentary rush of air that caused a loud whooshing sound as the ship quickly slipped beneath the waves. A quick look around confirmed there were no other lifeboats, and that they were the only survivors.

***

The sun bore down on them relentlessly as they bobbed on the waves for days. Their course was left to the winds and the currents.

Kami kept count of the days by notching the bench in the bow of the boat with a knife one of the deckhands had given her. After a week, their meager rations of biscuits and water were gone, and they resigned themselves to their fate.

But early the next morning, Kami spotted a fishing boat on the horizon and began frantically waving her arms. The First Mate, once he realized what Kami was doing, fired off the boat's emergency flair, which finally caught the attention of the fishermen, who rescued them.

Seeing the poor condition of the survivors, the fishermen provided a light meal and warm bunks in which to rest and sleep, before turning the boat towards their home port.

***

The next day as the fishing boat plowed the restless waves, Koshu entered the galley and found the Captain drinking tea. When he noticed her he smiled, "Did you sleep well? How are you feeling?"

"I slept like the dead and I feel lucky to be alive. Thank you for rescuing us. You have no idea what we have been through," Koshu stated as she leaned against the bulkhead, not having been invited to sit.

"Sit and have some tea. There are some biscuits and honey. When you are up to it, there will be some fish soup," the Captain stated.

"The tea and biscuits will be fine for now, thank you," Koshu replied gratefully.

"Are the children doing well?" he asked.

"They are sleeping soundly and after I have some tea and a few biscuits, I think I will join them again," Koshu shared as the Captain poured her a cup of tea. She dripped a small amount of honey on a biscuit before devouring it greedily.

"So," the Captain began, "where was the ship you were on headed?"

"We were headed for Hiroshima. I live there and I cannot wait to get home. I plan to stay in my garden until the snow falls. I want nothing else to do with war," Koshu stated in uncharacteristic firmness.

The Captain sat with his eyes focused on the table. He didn't make eye contact with Koshu until she asked, "What is wrong?"

The Captain looked up, presenting a somber face. His eyes were sad and he was frowning slightly. "You could not have known," he stated.

"No. We've been adrift for eight days. What is it?"

"You will not be going home, I'm afraid. You will never go home again," he stated in a near whisper.

"What do you mean? Why can I not go home?" Koshu asked.

The Captain looked directly into Koshu's eyes. She could see the sorrow in them as he spoke. "Hiroshima is gone."

"Gone?" Koshu gasped. "What do you mean gone?"

"The Americans bombed it today," he stated, then paused as Koshu sat staring at him. He wasn't sure how to explain it. How can one explain something that never existed until now and one didn't fully understand? How can he explain how an entire city had been destroyed, killing more than a hundred thousand people in an instant?

"They used some new weapon. We're told it destroyed the city and everyone in it." Then he added as an afterthought-one that was quite morose. "If Hiroshima was your destination, it was lucky for you that your ship was sunk. If not, you would have been killed in the attack with all the others."

Koshu was stunned. She didn't want to believe it. "My garden." She stated out loud. "My beautiful garden is gone?"

The Captain nodded. "I've been told the entire city is gone. All gone." The Captain repeated. "It is utter devastation."

Koshu sat silent as small tears began to drip down her cheeks. "Where will we live?" she uttered after a few moments.

"I've heard that displaced people," the Captain replied, the words sounding cold and callous, "are being sent to refugee camps in other cities. I guess we can take you to the nearest city."

"And where would that be?" Koshu inquired, hoping it wasn't too far from what she had known as home and hoping it would be almost as beautiful.

"Nagasaki, I believe," replied the Captain. "With luck, we should be there in a few days."

Mystified and perplexed, I lowered the stereopticon once again. I had to find out where he found it.

I was about to ask, Jeb when he cut me off in mid breath. "I bet you like secrets, huh?"

"Yes," I answered. "In fact..."

"The secret to immortality," he added with a sly grin.

"I...I..." I began to stutter.

He raised a knurled hand to my face to silence me and said, "Then you'll like this one." He quickly slipped a slide into the viewer.

I tilted the stereopticon towards the light once again and there, as before, right before my eyes, the slide came to life.

The first scene was that of a large stately mansion that filled the screen, then quickly switched to show a large modern kitchen and an elderly man in an apron. He had gray hair and a big, bushy gray mustache. He was standing at the counter, apparently preparing to serve a meal. Then the scene expanded to show a beautiful middle-aged woman standing several feet away, drinking a large glass of wine. She appeared to be uninterested in the man or the meal...

A SACRIFICE FOR YOUTH

"I'm going out," the woman affirmed as she put down her wine and started to walk away, without waiting for the man to comment about her leaving.

"Where are you going, Colleen?" her husband, Stephen Duncan, asked.

"I'm going to visit a sick friend. I won't need any dinner." Colleen informed him.

"Oh, I had been hoping we could spend the evening together." Stephen then quickly redirected the conversation. "So which friend is it tonight?" he asked curtly.

"Sandy. She's the one with the bad case of psoriasis-remember? It just over took her suddenly and she's really quite the mess. Why it's all I can do to console her," Colleen lied-badly.

"Surely you can stay for dinner. It's your favorite, sesame beef with noodles," he explained.

"Put it in the fridge. If I'm hungry when I get home, I'll eat it then," she stated brusquely and was gone from the room before he could reply.

Stephen slid the plates back from the edge of the counter, wiped his hands off on a dishtowel, then grabbed the bottle of burgundy from the cabinet shelf next to where he was working. He poured himself a large glass of the red liquid, took a deep drink and sighed loudly, resigning himself to the fact that he'd made a terrible mistake.

"You do know where she is going, don't you?" A young man spoke from the hallway leading into the kitchen. He had apparently been listening to their conversation.

"It's not polite to eavesdrop and yes, I'm not a complete idiot, Peter," Stephan responded, then took another large swallow of his wine.

"Dad, she is playing you for a fool. I don't know how you can let her get away with it," he berated his father. He stepped past him and picked a piece of meat off one of the plates and ate it. "Hmmm…good."

"I'll admit I was foolish when I decided to marry her. I gave her the freedom to do as she chose because I wanted her to be happy and because she is so much younger than me…"

"And you're just an old man," Peter snidely interjected.

His seventy-two year old father simply nodded.

"Why do you let her run rough shod over you? Why did you even marry her for that matter? It's as plain as day she's only here for the money."

Stephen looked out the floor to ceiling windows of the kitchen's dining area that overlooked a large expanse of manicured lawn leading down to the lake.

"I was lonely after your mother died," he replied as he ran a hand over his balding head - a nervous twitch he'd developed in the last year or two. "I had wanted companionship more than a sex partner and I thought Colleen was it. I thought I could make her happy. I thought she was happy when I asked her to marry me," he whispered as he hung his head and slowly shook it from side to side. "I was wrong, so wrong. I was fooled by her talk of family and of growing old together. I can see now, she's is just after the money."

"So divorce her. You have the pre-nup, right?" Peter replied.

His father nodded, then changed the subject. "This was supposed to be a back-to-college dinner for you."

"Don't sweat it, Dad. It's probably for the best."

Peter patted his father's shoulder in a small attempt to console him. "Besides, I was hoping to catch an earlier flight. The one Marie is on. You know, fly back together and all."

A smile crossed the old man's face, making his bushy mustache crinkle. "So how are you two doing? Wedding bells soon?"

"Still hoping for grand kids sooner than later?" Peter chuckled.

"Can't fault an old man for hoping," his father retorted.

Peter hugged his Dad and said, "I'll call you when I get in." Then he added, "Don't let Colleen destroy you, cut her loose as soon as you can deal with it. Then focus on the things that you've enjoyed in the past, like working with the library or the museum."

Peter's eyes lit up. "Say, have you finished cataloging grandpa's materials he left to the museum? If not, finish that up and try not to think about Colleen."

"How'd I get such a wise son?" Stephen asked.

"His mother raised him right," Peter retorted jokingly, since they both knew dad had spent Peter's formative years traveling the world on business.

"I wonder if I can ever find another woman like your mom," Stephen mused rhetorically.

"You might try talking with some of mom's friends," Peter suggested as he headed out the door.

Stephen finished his wine, poured another, and picked at his meal. He then headed down into the basement with a second bottle of burgundy, intent on sorting the materials his father had left to the local museum.

The museum had been more than patient and he knew it was time for him to fulfill his father's wishes and get it over with. The issue of Colleen would still be there tomorrow.

Stephen's father was Joseph Duncan, a noted anthropologist who had collected numerous antiquities over his many years of wandering around the globe. He was also an extremely smart man who had, while wandering globe, kept an eye open for investment possibilities and in doing so built a huge investment firm. He'd managed to successfully combine his two favorite pastimes, the search for man's past and the need to be financially independent. This way he might have both the time and the money to continue searching.

Stephen had inherited his father's drive in business but not his desire to traipse around the world looking for bits and pieces of man's past. In fact, it seemed that life had passed so quickly that he hadn't ever really developed a desire to do anything else but build a business.

His efforts had been rewarded though, for he was the CEO and Chairman of the Board of the largest private equities firm in the world. His son didn't have to work a day in his life, though he had chosen to seek degrees with only modest help from his father. Peter's self-reliant streak provided Stephen with a great deal of pride.

That train of thought brought him back to the issue with Colleen. How could he have been so foolish as to believe a forty-year-old woman could be satisfied with a seventy-year-old man? He had completely misjudged her, discovering only after the wedding that she was a selfish, self-centered woman-the epitome of a gold digger.

In a rare moment of clarity, his son had nudged him just enough to include a pre-nup in their marriage contract. The pre-nup precluded her from receiving more than a specified amount noted in the contract, a small percentage of Stephen's pre-marital estate upon his death, with the bulk going to his children to split equally.

Perhaps it was the only thing he had done right in regard to Colleen. He knew he'd have to make a decision soon regarding her and it depressed him to admit he had failed so miserably. He had completely misgauged the age difference and despite his immense wealth, he could do nothing to stop the march of time.

His thoughts turned back to the task at hand and, to his surprise, the cataloging took him several hours and a second bottle of burgundy to complete. His father had left hundreds of small items that he had acquired while rummaging through dusty, godforsaken villages or caves, hundreds of miles and hundreds of centuries off the well beaten track of modern man.

As dawn was breaking, he opened the last small crate. It appeared empty except for the packing paper. Knowing there had to be something his father had sealed inside the box besides packing paper, he rummaged around until his hands bumped into a small object.

It was a book – just a small book.

When it was finally released from the packing materials he was surprised yet again to see that it was a leather-bound notebook. There was a raised drawing or pictogram on the front of it. After looking at it for several seconds Stephen decided it was an abstract drawing of some sort. What it was meant to represent was beyond him. It looked almost like a flower with the head and shoulders of a man protruding from the center of it.

The pages of the notebook were yellowed with age and tattered along the edges. Just one look told him it was old. Very old.

The leather cover had been sewn on by hand using what appeared to be thin strands of leather. The pages themselves were made of parchment. The notes inside were obviously made by hand. They were clear and distinct, elaborate and utterly beautiful. He had never seen writing like this before, so it was lucky that dear old dad had provided a detailed translation of the squiggly lines and ornate symbols. He thumbed through his father's translation, which seemed to be instructions regarding a recipe of some sort.

Upon reaching the end of the translation, it was clear there was something missing-a final step and/or ingredient. He quickly thumbed back through the front pages and discovered he had missed something the first time through. The first two pages were stuck together.

He carefully tried to pull them apart, but stopped when it became apparent they would tear if he continued.

What to do?

He remembered his father had kept a toolbox that was filled with the instruments of an archeologist. After a moment of concentration, he recalled where he had placed it.

He retrieved the toolbox from the bottom of a nearby pile and opened it up, only to stare into it as if he knew what he was doing. He hadn't a clue. He needed something that would help him pry the two pages apart without destroying them. After a moment, he spied what looked to be a scalpel.

He quickly snatched it up and gently began slicing through the crud that had built up on the edge of the two pages. He worked slowly and methodically, just like his father had shown him many years ago. The pages popped open after his second pass, and he was rewarded with more of his father's translation notes.

This translation was different than the other pages. At the top was a title, 'The Elixir of Youth'.

Was that the notebook's title, or simply Dad's interpretation of the book's contents? He dismissed the thought since there couldn't be such a thing. That was strictly the stuff of myth and fairy tales.

He knew his father believed that every myth was based in fact, something his father had made him memorize at a very young age. But Stephen had never believed it, as his father had and thus had no such illusions about life and the world. He was nothing if not extremely practical and pragmatic.

He set the book aside, intent on going to bed and getting a couple hours of sleep before dealing with the Colleen issue. But he found himself drawn back to the book he and sat staring at it for several minutes before giving in to his curiosity.

In addition to the title at the top of the first page of the translation, Stephen noticed a name and phone number to the left of the title that had faded nearly completely away. The lighting in the basement was fine for watching videos or playing pool but was rather dim for his old eyes to read by. He gathered up the notebook and the translation notes and headed back upstairs to the kitchen.

He sat down at the snack bar and turned up the lighting so that a spotlight shown right down upon the notebook in front of him. Using the magnifying glass he kept in the drawer under the counter for reading the fine print on the contracts he frequently had to review and approve, he was able to determine a name and phone number in the upper left corner.

He carefully used a fine point pen to outline the letters and numbers. The phone number was a local number, but he didn't recognize the name. He made a mental note to have someone check it out later that day.

Then he turned his attention to the final translations. As he read it through, he was filled with wonder. It described several plants found in faraway places as being critical to the elixir and of a place that was surrounded by nearly vertical escarpments, but failed to name the place or the country it was in.

So much for finding answers in the final bit of translation.

It left him with more questions than answers. The biggest one was the final step, which his father stated he was unable to complete, but failed to elaborate, as to exactly what the step was. It didn't sound like his father. His father was a bulldog once he had sunk his teeth into a mystery. He just couldn't imagine him ever giving up on anything.

Stephen took several more sips of wine that had accompanied him all night, as he watched the sun rise over the house and send forth its rays to sparkle upon the crystal surface of the lake. It was early, too early to make the call that he was now anxious to make, but he also wanted to know what had stopped his father, the unstoppable force of nature, in his quest for…for what? Immortality? Would the phone number in the book provide any answers?

The words 'The Elixir of Youth' crossed his mind as he picked up the book once more and fingered the raised pictogram on the cover. He could see it now. It was a symbol of being reborn. His father must have actually believed he had found a way to cheat death.

To become young again.

But he had abandoned his quest at the last moment. Why?

* * *

Stephen showered, shaved, and dressed for a successful day investigating his father's final failed quest. He felt invigorated and not at all like the seventy-year-old who had been up all night. He then had the cook make him some eggs for breakfast. He decided to place the call right then and there. It rang several times before a man answered.

"Hello," the man answered.

"Good morning, I know it's quite early but I'm Stephen Duncan the son of…"

"Joseph Duncan," the man stated, cutting off Stephen in mid-sentence. "And you're looking for Mr. Pine."

"Why, yes I am, but how did you know?" Stephen asked.

"Then you've made the right call. I'm Mr. Pine," the man stated.

"But how…" Stephen stammered.

"How did I know you'd be calling? It's a long story. We should meet. I'll give you my address and would Thursday…"

"I could come right now," Stephen interjected, not wanting to wait to meet with the man.

"I can see the family resemblance from here. You are your father's son." There was a pause. "Of course, I have the morning open. Come right away," Mr. Pine stated, then provided the address and hung up.

Mr. Pine lived near the university and it took Stephen almost an hour to cross-town and ring the bell at the stranger's door.

Mr. Pine lived in one of the stone cottages in what had been the faculty housing section of the university many years ago. It was quaint, but very small by today's standards.

Stephen was nervous, which was so unlike him. He'd met with royalty and heads of state daily while working on his business, yet here he was about to meet a college professor and his palms were sweaty, his breathing labored.

The ride over had been filled with nostalgia, for as a child he had come to the university with his father on dozens of occasions, but he was never sure why they had come. Just that they had.

While father talked to one professor or another, Stephen would busy himself exploring the labs and libraries in which the meetings were held. He remembered his father saying that he should always go to the source rather than accept communication by letter or phone calls. He'd say, "You could learn a lot about the man you're dealing with when you look him in the eye." Those axioms had served Stephen well throughout his life-business and personal.

Stephen rang the bell and waited. He rang it once again and was about to knock when the door opened. The old wooden door creaked loudly as a small frail man stood back a step or two. After a moment of silence between them the old man spoke.

"Well, don't just stand there, come on in. I'd know you anywhere. You look just like your father, mustache and all."

The old gentleman turned and led Stephen into the living room. He took a seat by the hearth – a small fire was burning to chase off the chill of the late fall morning.

Stephen sat down in an overstuffed chair on the other side of a coffee table. He couldn't help but notice that the man's hands were curled with arthritis and he looked to be in a great deal of pain.

"I take it you're Mr. Pine, or would that be, Professor Pine?" Stephen asked.

"Did you take one of my classes? I think I would have remembered if you had," he said, not expecting an answer. "I was the Dean of the Anthropology Department, way back when."

"No. I never was a student here."

"Oh. Anyway, your father was quite generous over the years in return for what had actually been minor services on my behalf, aiding him in his quest for artifacts."

"He was quite the explorer. So is that how you knew my father?" Stephen asked, trying to be polite, though he just wanted to ask his questions and go.

When Professor Pine didn't respond immediately, Stephen spoke up again. "I was cataloging my father's collection and I came across…"

Professor Pine interrupted Stephen.

"A small leather notebook. Inside you found a translation of the ancient text that your father wrote and you're wondering what it is," he stated succinctly.

"Yes, but how did you know? I mean, you said you knew I would call and now you know exactly why I'm here," Stephen inquired. "How?"

"It's no mystery, Stephen. I was the man who helped your father discover what language the notebook was written in and then I helped him decipher it. I was the man whom he came to when he met with bitter disappointment having found the final step was impossible for him to take. We kept in touch over the years and when he became ill, we both knew when you went through his things you would find my name and number. We knew you'd want to know why he was unsuccessful in his quest and that you'd turn to me for answers. I'm afraid though, I cannot help you."

"Why?"

"You see, your father never shared exactly why he abandoned his quest. He'd followed the instructions to the letter and had gathered all of the other ingredients but when he had finally prepared it all and was ready to take the last step, he stopped."

The professor began to reminisce about himself and his father when Stephen asked, "I don't mean to be rude professor, but what can you tell me about the elixir?"

"Well, I can tell you that the ingredients came from around the world at great expense. Most were edible plants that your father harvested personally, at great risk. Even though he was unable to complete the transformation to 'The Elixir of Youth,' the mixture had surprising properties of its own. Both he and I took the mixture yearly and firmly believe that it is the reason we had both enjoyed such long lives. I'm ninety-eight years old. Most of my family died off in their sixties."

"It's sad, the elixir was used up five years ago and with no notes, other than the notebook from which to recreate the elixir, we started aging far faster than was natural, if only we hadn't taken the elixir to begin with," the old Professor stated remorsefully.

"Interesting, but where did my father go to find the last ingredient for the elixir?" Stephen pressed.

"That too I'm afraid I cannot say. You see, the last ingredient may have been a step to follow in the preparation. Both your father and I worked on narrowing down the field of choices as to the location of the great escarpment, the location of the final ingredient mentioned in the notebook. But it was he, alone, who traveled to each of the locations and finally discovered which one was the correct one. The only clue he shared with me, beyond the vague description of the area, was the rumor of a Sage who knew what the ingredient was and where it could be found. He never shared anything else with me. He felt it was far too great a secret to risk accidentally sharing it with the wrong person."

"Do you still have the list of locations?" Stephen asked.

"No, your father insisted that I turn over every piece of the research we worked on in regard to the elixir and he then claimed to have destroyed it all. Again, because it was too dangerous to risk the secret of the elixir being discovered by the wrong person."

Stephen pulled the notebook from his pocket and laid it on the table in front of the Professor.

Immediately, the Professor stopped talking and stared at the notebook.

Finally Stephen, sensing the Professor's tension, spoke up. "I was hoping that maybe seeing the notebook would help you remember something I could use to understand why my father failed to complete his quest and help me, perhaps, to complete it in his stead."

"No!" Professor Pine snapped. "Burn the damn book! Your father was right. It is too dangerous. If you must know, it was me whom he wished to shield the secrets from. I am, according to him, the type of person who should not learn the final ingredient. Your father spoke of it as if opening a door to great evil."

The Professor spouted, sounding half crazed and looking the part. "It was an obsession of your father to discover the secrets of the notebook. It took him twenty years and most of his first fortune to find the answers and only a moment to walk away. That was your father, pure of heart. I doubt I could have walked away and who knows where that might have led us all."

"I'm sorry to have upset you, Professor. I only wanted to get a little help from you. I didn't mean or intend to create such a reaction from you."

"It's evil, I tell you, evil!" the old Professor screamed as he struggled to his feet and walked to the far side of the room, where he turned his back to Stephen, clearly distancing himself from the notebook.

"If you don't care to help me, I guess I understand, but there's no need for all this drama," Stephen snarled, having taken offense at the man's outburst and behavior.

The Professor waved his hand dismissively, without turning around.

Stephen then stood, snatched the notebook off the coffee table, and walked out.

"Don't pursue the secret!" the Professor yelled out as the door closed behind Stephen. "It is evil and will destroy you. Your father was right to hide the secret away. Don't pursue it!"

Stephen sat in his car for the longest time. He was thinking about what the Professor had said and how his father had abandoned the search right when he'd discovered the final answer.

Why would he do that? There had to be a powerful reason.

The Professor seemed to think it was because the elixir was evil, but Stephen didn't believe anything inanimate could possess human qualities. It was more likely that mankind might try to use the elixir for evil purposes. But if he kept it secret, there was little chance mankind could exploit it.

The Professor's warning had done little to dissuade Stephen from taking up his father's quest. In fact, he was now even more curious as to what it was his father couldn't bring himself to do to complete the elixir. He had succeeded in collecting everything else needed to prepare the elixir, so why not follow through?

That was when Stephen decided he had to know why his father had failed to complete the project. He'd simply follow the instructions, as his father had done, only he'd complete the final step.

Stephen pulled away from the curb, making mental notes on what he'd need to prepare the elixir. The list was long, and he realized some of what he needed could only be obtained from very dangerous parts of the world.

Then his thoughts turned to Colleen, his wife.

'Wife' was an interesting term. Although she was his wife, by title, she was hardly so in spirit. He needed to provide her with some sort of story to keep her focused on something other than what he was actually doing.

He decided to tell her he was working on a new endeavor that would make them both extremely wealthy. That should satisfy her greed and keep her from pestering him about what he was doing and where he was going. He'd give her small gifts of jewelry and gold coins when he returned from each trip to assuage her curiosity and foster the idea he was creating more wealth.

Who knows, perhaps he'll discover the secret, be able to perform the task and extend his life indefinitely as a young and virile man! After all, it was 'The Elixir of Youth.'

* * *

Immediately upon returning home, Stephen contacted his travel agent and began his quest. He gave Colleen his story of why he was leaving on these trips, and she seemed to accept his small lie.

Colleen was still sleeping when he left on the first of a hundred trips he'd need to take. He left her a note telling her that he would be gone for many days.

It was while he was abroad that he had thought about the need for a secure, private work area. He thought about renting space away from the house, but decided instead to truly follow in his father's footsteps. That would be to use the old cottage at the far end of the property as his laboratory, just as his father had.

In fact, his father had built the cottage specifically as a proper place to conduct his work.

Stephen no longer remembered if the cottage was even in useable condition or if it was still locked and secure as it had been the last time he'd been there, some twenty-five years ago.

He went to his father's old desk in the basement and rummaged through it, looking for the key. He found it buried in the back right corner of the lowest drawer under a handwritten note stating the pool needed to be cleaned. He thought about all the strange things you'd find rummaging around in an old desk and when you rummaged about the world as well.

When he arrived at the cottage, the place was clearly showing its age. But, because it was built mostly of stone, it still was quite habitable.

It was a struggle to get the door unlocked. Having been unused for years, the lock must have collected dust and dirt in the tumblers, making their movement difficult, if not nearly impossible. After several minutes, he was finally successful and stepped inside the cottage.

He shined the flashlight he brought with him around the large open space. It had served as his father's laboratory and, despite its obvious age, looked to be in useable condition with just a little cleaning.

His first task was to find the circuit breakers and switch them on. He wasn't even sure if the power lines still ran to the cottage or if his father had them removed. He'd need power for the light and for the freezer in which he would store the ingredients until he was ready to prepare the elixir.

He found the circuit breakers in a closet next to the freezer and switched them all on. There were a few sparks and some strange popping sounds but after a moment everything appeared to be working. He quickly tucked his first collected and prized ingredient in the small walk-in freezer and turned his attention to the cottage's condition now that he could view it better.

He could see the skylight was intact and, with a little cleaning, would make a perfect source of daylight illumination, for the cottage had no overhead lighting. Only wall sconces. With the lights on, he could also see several large tables his father had used. They were still in place and with a little cleaning would work just fine to prepare the elixir.

Over the next several months, Stephen had several large shipments of beakers, glass tubing, Petri dishes - as well as pots and pans - delivered to the old cottage. His household staff insured the crates were moved inside, but were not to unpack them per his instructions. All they knew was that he had some things shipped to the cottage.

During this time he made dozens of trips, some just overnight and a few that lasted for a week or more. Where his father had to ride horses or camels for days to reach the sites where he could acquire the special ingredients, Stephen simply chartered a helicopter and accomplished the same task within hours. Where his father had to search through jungles and deserts, guessing at the locations, Stephen searched satellite imaging and knew exactly where to go, before he even left on the trip.

After each trip, he dutifully provided his unfaithful wife with some valuable trinket from a far off land as a token of his affection for her. It soothed her ego and he knew it kept her complacent.

He thought he had diminished her curiosity, but he was mistaken.

She was even more curious than when he first began his quest. Despite his request that she not discuss any of his travels or purchases with anyone, she felt she had to tell someone or she'd just burst.

The person she chose to confide in was her current lover. He was a young, handsome, virile and sexually exciting tennis pro at the country club - by the name of Josh Douglas. Josh was everything Stephen wasn't. After having shared her husband's secret, what little she knew, Josh began his own speculations as to what could possibly be in the crates piling up at the cottage.

While Stephen continued his travels, Josh began building what appeared to be a deeper relationship with Colleen. At his prompting, she agreed to finally break into the cottage to see what Stephen was hiding there.

After all, Colleen had said Stephen claimed it was more valuable than gold. As proof, Colleen showed Josh all of the trinkets made of gold, platinum, silver and diamonds that Stephen had given her stating, "It must be very valuable, far more then gold and silver, for he gives all of the gold and silver to me."

Josh was very impressed by the volume of gifts Stephen had lavished upon Colleen. It was a small fortune and he was determined to make sure he got his share of it.

"So what has he told you about his travels?" Josh asked, trying to discover a clue about what her husband was up to.

"What could be more precious than gold?" Colleen asked.

"I don't know, but we're going to find out," Josh stated confidently.

"How are we going to do that? He's so secretive," Colleen shared. "He hasn't told any of the servants and he keeps the cottage locked up tight."

"There's ways to find out. The easiest would be to get into the cottage and open the crates. Are you up for that?" Josh asked.

"We'll need to be careful. He might have security alarms on the cottage. He'd be real mad if he caught us," Colleen replied without directly answering Josh.

"You said he had you sign a pre-nup that dealt with his wealth prior to your marriage. What about the wealth he accumulates after the marriage?" Josh inquired.

"Oh, my attorney assured me that any new wealth he should acquire after the marriage, upon his death, would be mine alone," she remarked greedily. "His damn children won't get that. I wouldn't be surprised if he spends all of their inheritance, at the rate he's spending money on this new venture."

"So if he is acquiring new wealth, it's yours. But if you don't know what it is or where to find it, he could keep you from getting your fair share."

Colleen thought a moment. "Stephen is leaving for another trip tonight. We can try to get into the cottage after the servants go home."

"Then it's tonight," Josh agreed, rubbing his hands together in anticipation.

* * *

Where his father had needed years to find and collect the ingredients to make the elixir, Stephen had managed to gather all of them, more than a hundred in total, within six months. Like his father, Stephen had spent a large sum of money collecting the ingredients and now he was ready for the final ingredient or step. The one his father had been unwilling to partake of.

As a precaution against losing the notebook, Stephen had it copied, and he carried only the part of the book that dealt with the current item he went searching for. Not only did the copy help protect the book, it helped protect Stephen in his travels. By having only the few pages dealing with the single ingredient, he could claim that he had no idea why he was looking for it. He was just a hired hand sent to find it by some guy at a corporation in the States.

The ruse had saved his life more than once over the six months he'd been searching. Many of his guides had turned out to be little more than mercenaries seeking an easy payday.

After retrieving the notebook from the fire resistant box he'd hidden in the floorboards of the cottage, he gathered up the pages dealing with the last ingredient, the final step, and then returned it for safekeeping.

The comment about the Sage was in the margin of the translation, but not in the original notebook. Apparently, his father had discovered the information about the Sage from another source, but made no reference to it.

Further down the page in the margin was a second note. This one was about a small ancient kingdom in Southeast Asia. It gave no name. Just map coordinates.

Stephen checked Google Earth and found the coordinates were deep in the jungle of Myanmar, formerly Burma. Further checking revealed that the area was very mountainous and heavily forested. There were no roads, no cities, no rivers of any size, basically no access to the area other than by foot. There were no specific pictures, just a general description of the area as reported by a Dutch explorer in the 1800's. The man claimed to have been there and had met with the Sage, who was the de facto ruler of the area and claimed to be several hundred years old.

Stephen smiled broadly. The age was the key. The handful of other places that might fit the description in the notebook had no mention of a Sage. The fact that his father had written it in the margin and it was mentioned in the only report ever made by a westerner about the area had to be significant. He knew then where he would begin his search for the final ingredient.

But there was one major challenge. The area was embroiled in a civil war.

As he packed for the trip, he couldn't help but continue wondering why his father would travel to such a remote place and then refuse to follow the instructions of the Sage and complete the elixir.

He was becoming obsessed with needing to know why.

Everything he had believed about his father said he would never quit, never just give up, no matter the hardship. By the time he had reached this point in his quest, he'd battled man and beast for twenty years. Perhaps he had killed to fulfill his quest. Yet he had walked away. Abandoning his dream at the moment he had it within his reach!

It was the chiming of the clock in the hallway outside his room, 6:00 a.m., that drew him back from his ruminations about his father, and Stephen felt an overwhelming need to be prudent on this trip. He was headed into one of the most dangerous corners of the world and he wanted to succeed in his quest-not die trying.

He planned to buy a dozen gold coins when he arrived in Hong Kong and pick up a side arm there for the trip. He'd sew the coins into the seams of his pants and field jacket for concealment and find a suitable handgun with enough stopping power for protection. A 40 cal. Sig-Sauer handgun with five extra clips would do just fine.

When he had finished packing, he stopped in Colleen's room to tell her goodbye. Why he had ever agreed to her wish for separate bedrooms, he'd never know. Perhaps it was his desire to please her or to just make her stop pestering him about it. She claimed it was because he was always getting up and going to bed at odd hours that interfered with her sleep. But he knew in his heart it was because she didn't want him knowing when she got home on her nights out, and he didn't really want to know either.

He leaned over her and kissed her cheek, whispering he was off again and this time he might be gone just a bit longer than usual. He told her not to worry and promised to give her another exotic gift upon his return.

She mumbled, "Be safe," and rolled over pretending to sleep.

Stephen crept quietly from the room and closed the door behind him.

Alone again, Colleen rolled over and stared at the ceiling, contemplating the scheme she and Josh had worked out. The last of the servants left at 9 PM each evening and by 10 she and Josh would know Stephen's well-guarded secret.

* * *

Stephen arrived in Myanmar two days late. He'd been delayed in Hong Kong when his first application for an entrance visa was turned down. It was only after he had the company's attorneys contact the State Department and throw a little weight around that approval was given. It turned out all it took was a small contribution by the company to the ruling political party, and the visa was approved within hours.

The State Department official who delivered the approved visa warned Stephen of the dangers in Myanmar and suggested he postpone his visit indefinitely. Stephen ignored the young man and flew into Yangon, Myanmar the very next day. He then took a helicopter to the village, Lashio, arriving at dusk-it was the closest to the steep valleys formed by the escarpments described in the notebook.

From there, he had a two-day walk to the area of the escarpments--or it could be a month or a year-if he didn't get good information to start with and a guide he could trust.

He was to meet his guide at the only hotel for a hundred miles in any direction. It was named the Long House Bar. Clearly an American had been here and left his mark upon the community. It was built like so many of the longhouses that the local people had used as housing for centuries. This housed a fully stocked American-style bar and it sat on a small hill which dominated the village.

The man he was supposed to meet was Michael McMasters, a British archeologist.

"You McMasters?" Stephen asked to a man seated in front of the bar.

The Brit nodded and replied, "I assume you're Duncan."

"Yes, I am."

"So what brings you to the armpit's asshole? I don't recall there being any worthwhile ruins to investigate within a hundred kilometers."

"I'm here to explore the legend of the Sage," Stephen stated. McMasters immediately became agitated.

"Whoa mate," McMasters growled and then, in a hushed voice while nervously scanning the room, he said, "Let's not advertise the fact, OK?"

"What? Why?" Stephen asked quietly, taking his cue from McMasters.

McMasters looked about the bar once more, then waited for the bartender to bring Stephen his drink and move off before continuing. "The Sage is a touchy subject with the locals. They say he is very old and very evil. They say he lives up on one the cliffs around here somewhere and that every ten years he comes down and kills the first male he meets who is of the age of manhood. He kills them in the most vicious of ways. They say he chops off the heads and then drinks their blood. Personally, I don't think he really exists. I think he's just the local's version of the boogeyman."

"Well, that's what I'm here to find out. To prove it one way or the other," Stephen stated as he took a swig of his drink.

"That's going to be hard to prove, right? How do you prove a myth? Do you have a camera crew?" McMaster's asked.

"No, I'm the advance man. If I can find someone who will tell me where to find the Sage and he's actually there, then a crew will be sent in to film it all for the Discovery Channel."

"That's quite the outfit. I've seen programs from time to time when I'm in the bigger cities. Of course you have to watch out for rebels."

"Rebels?" Stephen questioned.

"Yes, rebels. The local tribesmen have rebelled against the government because they are letting outsiders into the area to search for gold and other precious metals. The mountains here are chuck-full of gold, silver, copper, and a half dozen other valuable minerals. The locals have mined precious metals for centuries as a way of life and it has always been their private concern. But now the government has been allowing multinational mining operations to come in and dig up whatever they want, wherever they want. The rebels have lodged complaints but they've fallen on the deaf ears of the politicians who are lining their pockets with money from the multi-nationals."

McMasters stared in his drink. "It's become a real blood bath as of late. I stay in town, myself, not being a local. I'm known around here but it's just too dangerous. All it would take is one rumor about me scouting for some outside mining company and I'd end up with my throat slit. Rumors are as good as the truth around here."

"I'll have to be careful then, but I'm still going to look for the Sage," Stephen stated in reply as he finished his drink.

"Know the language, do you?" McMasters asked sarcastically.

Stephen wondered if it would be prudent to lie, knowing he'd be found out in short order. "Actually, no, I don't," he admitted.

"For a few bucks I could ask around for you." McMasters, like everyone else in this backwater burg, was angling for cash.

"How much?" Stephen asked.

"Say a hundred?" McMasters asked hopefully.

"And what will I get for my hundred?"

"The location of the Sage, if he is around here. There are several hundred villages that all back up to big escarpments and he could be on anyone of them," McMasters stated.

"How did you know he was on one of the escarpments? I never mentioned that," Stephen asked, wondering if he was about to be taken.

"It's the legend. The legend states the Sage lives among the rocks on the escarpment, because when he was born that is where the people lived. They lived in caves up there. They repelled down from their homes when they had to and were quite safe from the marauding tribes that came into the jungle in search of slaves and gold like the multi-nationals are doing with their job offers and their never ending greed."

"So is there someone I should be paying for the privilege of searching for the Sage?" Stephen questioned.

"I'm not sure who that would be but I'll ask around just the same as for the location of the Sage. I'll get back in touch, say mid-morning?" McMasters suggested.

"No later than eleven. I want to get started on the search," Stephen stated, knowing mid-morning around here could mean anything.

"I'll try but no guarantees. The folks around here don't work on any schedule that I can ascertain," McMasters stated, and then held out his hand for the money.

Stephen dug through his pocket a moment and pulled out a fifty-dollar gold piece, handed it to McMasters and waited for his reaction.

"This is only half," McMasters stated, plainly annoyed by Stephen's action.

"Fifty up front and fifty when you get back to me," Stephen stated flatly, not giving McMasters anywhere to go with his complaint.

"How do I know you're good for it?" McMaster's snapped.

"The same way I know you'll follow through with your end of the deal. You'll just have to trust me."

"You're killing me. Just plain killing me," McMasters stated as he stood and walked away.

Stephen found his way to what was referred to here as his hotel room. It was a grass shack out behind the Long House Bar. Its amenities included a hammock and a wooden bench on which to set your suitcase or bag. There wasn't a clock or a phone, so Stephen assumed rightly, there wouldn't be any wake up call.

Stephen settled in after drinking a bottle of water and eating an energy bar he'd brought with him and was soon fast asleep. His watch had said it was after eleven in Hong Kong, but here he wasn't sure if he was an hour or two hours behind Hong Kong. It didn't matter, and he set the alarm for eight a.m. Hong Kong time.

Stephen dreamed of his father sleeping in this same hut and soon he'd be trekking through the same jungle as his father had done nearly forty years ago. With luck he'd know the final ingredient by nightfall two days from now and he'd know why his father had abandoned his quest.

Stephen also dreamed of Colleen. She was in the arms of another man and laughing at him.

He really did love her, but he'd been such a fool to have fallen for a woman so much younger. When he returned home and rejuvenated himself, he'd make one final attempt to convince her to change her ways. If she chose not to, then he'd divorce her and use his new vitality to woo another trophy wife.

One closer to his own age.

Suddenly, there was a loud bang - and then another.

To a sleepy Stephen, it sounded a lot like gun fire-which it was. Stephen jumped off the hammock and pulled the Sig-Sauer forty caliber from its holster, just as another round of loud bangs, as though issued from a machine gun, echoed through the night.

He was about to venture a step forward when he thought he heard someone breathing-and froze in place.

That proved to be a mistake.

Stephen felt something strike the back of his head-hard-and down he went to his knees, seeing stars and colored swirls. He wasn't quite unconscious but close, that is, until the second blow landed on the back of his head and he blacked out.

***

Stephen woke to a bright light shining in his face and a headache that rivaled the worst migraine he'd ever had. He struggled to get fully awake for the longest time while listening to what he had thought was someone talking. But the more he listened, the more it sounded to be just gibberish.

Finally, he rolled on his side and opened his eyes. The room was spinning slowly and the edges of his vision were blurry. His first thought was, this didn't look like his hotel room. The wall he could see was a stucco wall without any paint on it and he was laying on a wide wooden plank with tree trunks underneath it for support. The floor was gray dirt and there were ants crawling about on what appeared to be a dirty dinner plate. He thought that was strange because he hadn't had any dinner last night.

He closed his eyes for what he had thought was a short period of time. However, when he opened them again, he was surprised to see the bright light had dimmed substantially, but someone nearby was still speaking the gibberish.

He decided to make a real effort to sit up this time. He pushed himself up with his right arm to a sitting position. That was a mistake. The room began to spin furiously. He felt nauseated and quickly laid back down on the bench.

Suddenly, there was a loud clanging sound, and he whipped his head around, as best he could, to see what caused the noise. There, just beyond a row of iron bars, was a small Asian man banging what appeared to be a large metal cup on the bars of what was clearly a prison cell.

Over the din of the clanging, the man yelled, in an Asian accent but broken English, "About time you wake up. Thought maybe hit you too hard. Thought maybe you dead."

From the man speaking, Stephen's eyes wandered upward to the ceiling, and he realized that there was a large hole there open to the sky. The hole was maybe twenty feet above his head and seemed centered between the cell containing the Asian man and himself.

"Where am I?" Stephen asked as he gingerly touched the large lump on the back of his head.

"You nowhere good my friend, nowhere good," the man stated through a toothless grin as he continued to clang the metal cup.

"Could you please stop banging that cup?" Stephen shouted. When the little man finally stopped, Stephen asked, "Where are we?"

"Prison."

"But why? What did I do?"

"You come to town and you have money. You American, folks back home pay to save you."

"Now I know I'm in trouble," Stephen stated loudly, trying to think fast. "I'm on my own. I have no family, no employer. My address back in the States is a post office box."

"You live in a box?" the man asked.

"It's just a place where people can send me letters." Stephen tried to keep it simple and then changed the subject. "So how long have I been here?"

"Most the night, then all day. It be night soon again," the man informed him.

"So why are you here?" Stephen asked.

"I got caught stealing food from them. I very good thief. First time I get caught. They say I have to work off what I owe them by stealing for them, otherwise they kill me. You have hard head. I try not to hit too hard because if you die, they get no money and things go bad for me. So I careful, hit just right, but you no go down, so I hit you again."

"You were the one who attacked me in my hotel room?" Stephen asked, not sure how to respond to that revelation.

"You should thank me. I do a good job. I hit you same place twice so as not crack you skull. No kill. Just knock out."

"Thank God for small favors," Stephen stated sarcastically. "So how long have you been here? You know, locked up?" Stephen decided to clarify the question after the little man gave him a strange look.

"I've been here long time, long time. Days and days. But not so bad. They feed me, send me women. I get to sleep all day and at night, I go with them to steal from mining camps and other villages. No one sees me, I very good," the little thief shared.

"Yes, you said that. Only been caught one time," Stephen retorted sarcastically.

"Yes, just one time." The thief smiled as though it was a major life accomplishment, then asked. "Why you come here?"

Stephen was quiet for several seconds as he debated whether or not he should share his mission there. He decided that if he were going to get out of here, he'd need help. So he told the little thief.

"I'm looking for the Sage. I'm told he lives on one of the escarpments in this area."

"Big area."

"So I'm going to need a guide. But first I have to get out of here. Do you think I can bribe the guard?" Stephen asked.

"No way."

"Why?"

"Cause you got to bribe me first."

"Why would I need to bribe you? You're a prisoner just like me."

"Not like you," the little thief stated. He stood up, walked over to the cell door, and pushed it open. He stepped out and smiled at Stephen. "I come and go sometimes, no problem. No like you."

Stephen did his best to get up and stagger to his cell's door. He pushed on it. It didn't open. He turned and staggered back to the wooden bench and sat down.

Just then, a large oriental man came around the corner and barked at the little thief in what Stephen could only comprehend as totally foreign. The little thief bowed, spat a mouth of fast talk back at the guard and backed into his cell, pulling the cell door closed behind him.

The large guard turned and gave Stephen a nasty look, then walked back around the corner.

"He no like you. You really stuck."

"I think I'll be able to bribe him," Stephen stated absently, as he leaned forward, placing his head in his hands.

What he wouldn't give for some aspirin, he thought.

"You need to bribe me. The guard no speak English," the little thief stated again.

"I don't think so. I'll just show the guard the money and he'll get the idea."

"No. He hit you over the head and take money."

"I don't think so. I'll get the message across," Stephen stated confidently.

"You speak the language?"

"That was a language you two were speaking?" Stephen taunted him.

"Very old. All the local speak it. But outsiders not so much. The Sage speak this language," the little thief stated, perking Stephen's interest.

"Oh. How do you know that?"

"People see and he speak to them. He no educated in missionary school like me, so what else could he speak?"

Stephen found it hard to argue with the logic, so he didn't.

"So how much of a bribe do you require?" Stephen asked, thinking he just might be able to use the little thief to get to the Sage as well as to escape prison.

"How much you have?" the little thief replied.

"I have enough," Stephen said derisively.

"I don't know. Guard very expensive. Me not so much."

"How much?" Stephen asked again.

"How much you have?" The little thief repeated his question.

"Oh, forget it. I'm not going to argue with you," Stephen stated tersely.

"What argue? I ask how much you pay and now you want to stay in prison?" He spat out what had to be a curse word or two in the gibberish he called a language.

"Ok, I'll pay you two hundred American to help me bribe the guard and another two hundred to take me to the Sage." Stephen figured that would be more than enough.

"Paper no good here," the little thief replied.

"I have gold."

"Krugerrands?" the little thief stated, mispronouncing the name of South Africa's collectible coins.

"Better. American Bald Eagle and Lady Liberty."

The little thief sat down and thought about it for a while. Then a smile broke across his face and he chirped, "Deal."

The bribing of the guard happened quickly. The little thief conversed with the guard for several minutes before saying it was a deal. He would let them go for five hundred American gold dollars, and held out his hand.

Stephen shook his head and told the thief to tell him that he didn't have the money on him. He'd hidden it back at the hotel.

This news didn't set well with the little thief. He turned to the guard and explained they had to go to the hotel to get the money.

The guard shouted angrily at the little thief but eventually it was worked out. For fifteen hundred dollars Stephen bought his freedom and hired a guide to lead him to the Sage.

* * *

Once back at the hotel, Stephen had his little 'friend' distract the guard for a few moments. He retrieved the gold from his clothing and then paid the guard his due.

Within minutes of having paid the guard off, Stephen and the little thief were following a well-worn path through the jungle that was supposedly leading them to the Sage.

"It best we not stay around village very long. We collect food to eat as we go. Lots of food out here," the little thief stated. He kept looking about as if concerned someone could be watching them.

"So how long will it take us to get there?" Stephen asked him.

"That depend on you."

"What does that mean?"

"You old man, maybe good shape, maybe not. It is long walk, two days at best time. We can stop and sleep or stop to rest now and then, is up to you. The more we stop, the longer it take. The more likely someone find us."

"Who would be looking for us?"

"Boss of guard who let us escape. The soldiers looking for rebels might find you, shoot just the same."

"You do know how to avoid them right?" Stephen asked, feeling real fear for the first time on this trip. Everywhere he looked was jungle. Thick, lush, and dangerous.

"Oh sure, can hide anywhere. But have to be careful not to become meal for tiger," the thief stated with a smirk.

"Do you have a weapon?" Stephen asked.

"I have my knives. I throw knives better than I shoot arrows. Plus I have this gun, big gun." The little thief said as he pulled Stephen's Sig-Sauer from under his shirt. "I think you can use this. I don't shoot gun before," he stated as he handed it to Stephen. The little thief then reached in his pocket and pulled out the five extra clips that had been in Stephen's travel bag.

Stephen took the weapon and clips and stuck them in his jacket.

They trudged through the jungle for two days and just before sunset, on the second day, they stepped into a clearing at the base of an escarpment.

The thief pointed straight up and said, "Sage, he live up there. Take path around and up in morning." He was pointing off to his right, but wasn't specific.

Stephen and the little thief made camp under a large leafed fern of some sort. When Stephen woke up he was glad they had, because it was raining fairly hard and the large leaves of the fern were keeping him dry.

He wished they could build a fire and could make a real breakfast because he was starved. All he had to eat was the fruit that the little thief had collected while they were walking yesterday afternoon. The fruit was fine but unlike the little thief, a couple pieces for him did not make a meal. Stephen needed at least twice the calories simply because he was twice as big. The fruit was just a snack to him.

After what had felt to be at least an hour, Stephen sat up and called out for the little thief. "Hey, thief, where are you?" He felt a bit strange calling him thief, but the little man never shared his real name with him.

After calling out on and off for another hour, Stephen realized the little thief had abandoned him. A quick check of his backpack and Stephen discovered that the little thief had lived up to his name. He'd stolen half of his remaining gold and silver. The little thief was indeed quite good because Stephen had been using the backpack as a pillow and he never noticed anything.

Stephen also remembered what the little thief had said last night about taking the path around and up in the morning. He began searching for a path that would lead him up the side of the escarpment. By the time he found the path, the rain had stopped and the sun was out, baking the jungle once again.

He followed the path that led off to his right and gradually climbed the escarpment. The escarpment wasn't quite as steep as it was where he had camped for the night, but it was taking every ounce of his strength to make the climb.

Finally, after three hours, he reached the Sage's lair. He wasn't sure what to expect, but he was not expecting to see the large steel door before him with its huge steel hinges anchored in the solid rock surrounding the cave's mouth.

Stephen waited several minutes to catch his breath before knocking on the door, for he had no idea what to expect next.

He pulled out his gun and held it slightly to his side, and knocked again. This time, he noticed the knocking echoed loudly in the narrow cave mouth. A few seconds later, he heard what sounded like large chains being pulled loose behind the door. There was a loud creaking sound and then the door slowly swung outward. There, in the open doorway, stood a figure that looked surprisingly familiar.

"It is good to see you make it," the little thief stated, as he turned and walked back into the cave.

"You're the Sage?" Stephen blurted out.

"No, I had to interpret for you, remember."

"But how did you get here?"

"I walk up path just like you. Now shut up and the Sage will see you." The thief beckoned Stephen to follow him further into the cave. They made a turn along the pathway to the left and then a few yards further they turned right, ending in a large room. It was filled with artwork, paintings and drawings, and a few pieces of furniture.

Another smallish oriental man, with grayish brown hair framing a bronzed face was sitting on a large cushion on top of a big flat boulder off to the side of the room. He was dressed like most of the locals in loose fitting cotton pants and a white short-sleeve shirt.

He had been reading something when Stephen and the little thief entered the room. He set his reading aside and looked up directly at Stephen. His eyes were dark, and the look he gave Stephen made him nervous. After a minute or so, the Sage turned to the little thief and said something in his native language that the little thief translated.

"Why have you come to see me, son of Joseph Duncan?" The little thief spoke for the Sage.

Stephen almost fainted. He'd told no one his name, let alone his father's name, and yet the Sage knew both.

"I've come to see you," Stephen stated, and the thief translated for the Sage, who looked Stephen over with a penetrating stare. Stephen thought the man looked wise and worldly, though he knew he had never been more than fifty kilometers from this spot. He wondered if he would look as wise a few hundred years from now.

The Sage spoke and the thief translated. "You are wondering just how old I am. I am more than 500 hundred years old. Your father wondered the same thing when he was here forty years ago. I was almost 500 hundred years old and he too carried a weapon."

Stephen had absently kept the gun in his hand when he'd entered the cave behind the little thief.

Again the little thief translated. "I can assure you, Mr. Duncan, if I had wanted to harm you, you would have never been allowed to make the climb up the path. So put your toy away and ask me the question that has driven you to travel across the world to find me."

Stephen slipped his gun back in his jacket, eyed the Sage a moment and then eyed the little thief. "I wish to know the final ingredient for the Elixir of Youth."

The old Sage grinned. Then he nodded his head several times before answering the thief with a flurry of gibberish.

The thief stood silent for several seconds after the flourish ended, as if he was struggling with how to translate the information just given him. "He says, you, like your father, have confused the language. For the last step or ingredient, as you call it, is not part of the Elixir. In fact, as he told your father, the wisdom of the elixir is in the arranging-not the mixing. The last step, as you call it, does not recommend that you do anything."

Stephen made a face as the Sage's answer ran through his mind. He couldn't comprehend the meaning of 'Not do anything.' So Stephen turned towards the little thief and blurted, "I don't understand."

The Sage, in turn, blurted out another flourish of gibberish and the little thief once more appeared to struggle with the translation for a moment.

"He says, the book tells you to come on this pilgrimage and it tells you that a certain ingredient is needed but it does not say you have to actually obtain it."

The little thief shrugged his shoulders and Stephen locked eyes with the Sage.

After a moment the Sage looked at the thief, who then continued with his translation.

"The idea of a needed ingredient is of your own invention and the procuring of the ingredient is of your own assumption as well."

The old Sage then leaned towards Stephen, and surprising Stephen, spoke in plain English. "Each process must go step by step. Here is the last." Then the wise old Sage quietly spoke six words in English - with complete clarity.

Stephen recoiled in disgust. Now he knew why his father had forsaken his quest.

* * *

Colleen and Josh were ready to implement their plan as soon as the servants had left. So, shortly after ten, they took the golf cart across the property to the old cottage. They circled the building, looking it over, running a flashlight over it searching for any security wires or cameras.

There were none.

Josh stopped the cart in front of the cottage and tried the door, but it was locked. There were no windows so Josh returned to the cart and gave the problem some thought. Just when he was about to suggest they go and get an ax from the gardeners shed, Colleen noticed there was an old ladder lying against the side of the cottage.

Josh nodded, grabbed the ladder and began to climb as Colleen stood and held the ladder steady at the bottom.

Once he reached the roof, he hesitated. It was an old wood shingled type and there were plenty of broken and missing shingles. Tentatively, he put his first foot onto the roof and tested his weight by leaning into it. The roof creaked, but it held his weight. Slowly he stepped forward, placing both of his feet on the roof, while still clinging awkwardly to the ladder. The roof creaked again, louder this time, but once again, it held his weight. Slowly, he worked his way across the rickety roof, doing his best to avoid the areas with missing shingles.

"What do you see?" Colleen called out.

"I'm not sure. I think I see a skylight."

"Can you get in that way?" Colleen inquired.

"Give me a minute and I'll let you know," Josh replied.

Upon reaching the skylight, Josh called out, "The skylight looks to be hinged. I'm going to try to get it open."

"Okay, be careful," Colleen shouted in reply.

Colleen really didn't care whether or not Josh was careful. She was too busy wondering exactly what they would find once inside. Any moment now she would know what her husband was hiding.

Suddenly, the sound of Josh screaming, "Ahhh" followed quickly by the sound of breaking glass, abruptly ended her musing.

"Josh!" she called out. "Josh!"

She stepped back from the cottage, trying to see what may have happened, but it was too dark. She walked around to the door again and tried it.

Still locked.

After waiting fifteen to twenty minutes nervously wondering what to do, she went back to the mansion where she rehearsed a story of the event, and finally called the authorities.

When the police arrived, they found the young man dead, lying in the center of the floor inside the cottage under the broken skylight. They questioned Colleen as to how she could have known there was anything amiss when the cottage was too far away to hear anything going on.

Colleen explained that she had seen lights flashing in the direction of the cottage as she looked out the windows on her way to bed. When they showed her a picture of the dead man, she simply shook her head and said she thought he might be one of the tennis pros at their club. The police assumed the young man might have heard something about all the crates being delivered there and thought he could make some easy cash by stealing and selling some of the stuff.

Because Colleen was the wife of one of the most respected members of the community and they could find no solid connections between Colleen and the dead man, they took her word for the whole situation. They closed the case and labeled it as a burglary attempt gone bad.

* * *

Stephen returned home, depressed and frustrated. He was such a fool to think he could cheat time and death. Only a real fool would believe there was any such thing as an 'Elixir for Youth'.

All the time and effort he'd expended was for nothing. He had wasted millions of dollars all because he was a desperate old man. No wonder his young trophy wife was out fooling around all over town.

Upon returning to his home, his anger and frustration seething within him, he went immediately to the cottage. Although he was alarmed at the yellow caution tape draped across the cottage doorway, he hesitated only for a moment. He'd find out later about the tape.

Something more important drove him forward.

He burst into the cottage where he took the kerosene he had stored there to use in the heater for warmth as he worked. He poured it over all the crates and the ingredients he had so carefully and expensively collected.

He paused and looked over the soon-to-be flaming sacrifice, then stepped outside the door and struck a match. He tossed it into the building and immediately, large flames burst through the door and the broken skylight. He hadn't made any attempt to recover the notebook from its hiding place in the floorboards. He was more than content to let it burn, too.

The servants were all-aflutter with Stephen's behavior and had gone to Colleen with the news he was home and of his mood. It prompted her to hurry to the cottage, where she found Stephen standing outside the building watching the fire grow.

Upon realizing she was standing behind him, he turned towards her and spouted, "I was a fool. All that I have worked for is for nothing. I sought to keep my quest a secret from you, so that I might surprise you and win back your heart but since I have abandoned my foolish project, I can now tell you exactly what it was I was up to."

He paused a beat in thought, then continued. "I was trying to produce, from a book that my father had owned, an elixir that would have made me young again. My father had tried the same thing but failed at the last moment, just as I have done. The final ingredient when taken as instructed will indeed provide the recipient with eternal youth. I have seen the proof with my own eyes. But I, like my father, could not bring myself to perform the final task."

"Final task," she asked, knitting her eyebrows together. "What task?"

"The whole process was so abhorrent and perverse that no civilized man would do it. My father had labeled it evil and rightly so. So as a last gesture to him and to save our family name, I am destroying all of the ingredients and the equipment needed to prepare the ingredients as my father should have done, many years ago."

"But what could possibly be so abhorrent that you would need to burn the cottage down?" Colleen inquired. "I don't understand. What is it exactly that you were up to and what was the final ingredient or step that you could not take?"

Stephen sighed deeply and then took Colleen in his arms and held her close so as to whisper in her ear. He uttered the six words that the old Sage told him. *"A young man must be sacrificed"*.

As the slide faded into black, I handed this mysterious machine back to old Jeb. He glanced quickly towards the kitchen and, feeling assured Helen was going to stay there for a while longer making dinner, he reached into his pocket and removed a previously hand-rolled cigarette. He propped it between his lips and lit it.

The old cowboy took a long satisfying drag and then slowly let out a cloud of blue smoke. In doing so he had created a bluish haze in the room that had added an unpleasant aroma to inviting smells of dinner emanating from the kitchen.

"Jeb, exactly where on earth did you find this thing?" I asked, handing the viewer back to him and hoping he'd tell me - because I wanted one.

Jeb flicked some ash off his cigarette and into his hand, then dumped it into his shirt pocket without answering me. He looked at me and gave me a mischievous grin." You really want to know?" he asked around the cigarette dangling from his lips.

"Yes, I really want to know." I stated, leaning forward as if he might whisper my request. His answer shocked me.

"Found them in a spaceship," he mumbled around his cigarette.

"A spaceship!?"

"Yeah. Found it while rounding up my herd one winter."

He went on to explain that while rounding up his horses, he noticed one of them digging in the muddy ground with its hoof. He walked over to the spot and saw the horse had uncovered some kind of silvery object. He dug around it and was able to extricate it.

He brought the small what he called - a spaceship -into the house and, after much work, he was able to pry open the object and found the slides.

"You telling me you found a UFO? That's quite a story Jeb. If you didn't want to tell me where you got it, you just could have said so." I chuffed.

"Son, I'm telling you it was real. A spaceship about five feet long - cigar shaped."

"Oh come on, Jeb, that doesn't make any sense. I suppose there were little green men inside it, too?"

Jeb took another long drag on his cigarette and, as he let it out, deepening the blue haze, he replied. "Nope. No little green men." He took another drag. "Anyway, Helen and I soon discovered the strange and wonderful properties of the slides and decided to keep them. The slides came in handy for entertaining an isolated and lonely couple in the winter of their years."

"Jeb, I chuckled, "you are quite the story teller. I pulled on my chin. "So...where's this spaceship now?"

"In the cellar."

"Would you mind if...?"

But Jeb interrupted me. "View some more," he more or less commanded, then reached into the silver box, pulled out a slide, and handed it and the device to me. Over the next hour, he handed me another. Then another. Then another....

MISSING LINK

Deacon Ignatius Ajo along with his graduate assistant, Deaconess Angelica Tonalea, sat impatiently waiting in the anteroom of the Abbott of the Ecclesiology Committee at the College of Cardinals offices for a decision on their latest research proposal.

The two fought off the desire to doze off under the hum of some power source entering the small little room. They were both fatigued after working eighteen-hour days, putting Ajo's proposal together for the review. Though anxious, it was a nice break to just sit there in the Abbott's office with its luminous walls providing a relaxing aura of light.

Sometime later, the door to the Committee's Chambers opened, rousing them from their dozing, and a page announced that the Committee would see them now.

Tonalea took a seat along the back wall of the room and Ajo stepped up to the railing facing the half moon conference table at which the nine Committee Members sat to deliberate scientific proposals. Ajo waited several moments for the Abbott to finish writing down some notes. The eight other members of the Committee remained silent. Finally the Abbott finished, cleared his throat and began.

"Your argument for this grant is intriguing," he noted, after a long study of Ajo's material. "But what makes you think you can succeed where others have failed?"

"As the proposal explains, Your Reverence, all of the other expeditions have failed because they were looking in the wrong places."

"But the Orion Arm?" The Abbott objected. "That is on the fingers, the outskirts of the galaxy. The Church has discounted that area as too primitive to host a civilization of the maturity to foster a civilization of such magnitude as ours."

"Yes, Your Reverence, I understand that it is a long held belief based on historical sources that our civilization has been centered for eons here in the central hub of the galaxy. But I believe that the authors of the historical text may have misinterpreted the data. After all, because of the historical data, we haven't ever sent an expedition to the Orion Arm. Perhaps it is time we did, if for no other reason than to confirm the historical text."

The Abbott shuffled the papers before him. "Now what about the Spheres you talk about in your proposal? These Ajo Spheres?" It was obvious from the tone of his voice that the Abbott took a dim view of Deacon Ajo naming the theory after himself. "You claim that their existence proves there is intelligent life and ergo civilizations on that arm of the galaxy?"

"Yes, Your Reverence." Ajo began talking fast, his excitement showing at the opportunity to explain what he believed was a breakthrough theory. "My theory predicts that every civilization in the Universe eventually runs out of energy on its home planet. Provided, of course, it survives long enough to do so, this event constitutes a major hurdle in a civilization's evolution, and that all of those who overcome this hurdle do so in precisely the same way."

Ajo then lowered his voice for emphasis and leaned forward at the rail and said, "They've all built a massive system of solar collectors surrounding their planets, making a shell, if you will." He leaned back, waited a moment to intensify the attention, and then continued in a quiet voice. "I call them Ajo Spheres and you can detect them with our long range telescopes. My hypothesis is sound, and if you want to find advanced alien civilizations, you need to look for signs of the Ajo Spheres."

"And that is exactly what we found," Tonalea jumped up and excitedly interjected, overstepping the bounds of her position as an observer. "On the Orion Arm of the galaxy, we found an Ajo Sphere." Ajo swung around and tried subtly to quiet her. Upon seeing Ajo's hand gestures, she sat back down and uttered an apology. "Sorry. Excuse me."

The Abbott sat quietly pondering Ajo's statement for several moments before he spoke up again. "The College of Cardinals will consider your proposal. We'll inform you of our decision within the month," the Abbott stated with an air of finality, dismissing the Deacon and his assistant.

* * *

Deacon Ajo and Deaconess Tonalea returned to their office on the far side of the campus. It was a long and quiet walk. Tonalea did not utter a word. She knew she had stepped out of bounds with her teacher and mentor.

Once they had arrived back at their office and had sat down, she said, "I'm sorry. I just got carried away in the moment." They both had heard the stories of good proposals being turned down because of the petitioner's lapses in protocol and she knew she might well have ended their chances with her outburst.

"It's a good proposal, Ajo replied. "The best proposal. I can't believe for a moment that they'd be so unyielding that they would deny our request because of your enthusiasm." He then turned to look out the window.

"Aside from my mistake, what do you think our chances are?" Tonalea just couldn't sit quietly, not for a second.

"They can test my theory themselves simply by looking at any number of known worlds that have within the past few decades managed to make the transition to complete solar power," Ajo ruminated out loud. "They always test each theory brought before them and when they do, they'll see my theory and the proposal are sound."

They sat silently contemplating their own thoughts for a dozen minutes or so, when there was a knock on their office door. It was a messenger.

He presented an envelope to Ajo, waited for him to sign the receipt, then left.

As Ajo turned around, Tonalea started asking questions. "Who sent it? Was it the Abbott's Committee? Is this a good thing it was decided so quickly or a bad thing? Did they approve us?"

Ajo held up his hand and waited for Tonalea to stop and when she did he said, "Yes, it's from the Committee. I haven't the foggiest idea about whether it is a good thing or bad thing. They have made their decision so fast. I'll open it, provided you remain quiet and let me read it in peace." Ajo curtly stated.

Tonalea remained silent for several seconds as Ajo began slowly tearing open the envelope. He then pulled out the plastic sheet inside and read the message there.

He read: *"The Abbott's Committee has approved your proposal and agrees to provide funding as needed to make the expedition to Orion's arm in search of an advanced civilization and the Law Giver."*

"So now what do we do?" Tonalea asked, thoroughly excited.

"Now we form the expedition!" Ajo exclaimed.

* * *

Over the next couple of months, Ajo and Tonalea gathered the supplies they needed and recruited a social archeologist, an anthropologist, botanist and of course, a zoologist, all approved by the Church.

With most of the preparations for the expedition completed, Ajo was faced with dealing with the last requirement of the Church - the priest that the Church assigned to the expedition.

"The Church of course will assign a priest," he told Tonalea. "He will be charged with converting whatever intelligent life we encounter." He added in a scornful tone, "It goes without saying that whatever we find will have to be vetted and approved by the Church."

* * *

Finally three months after receiving approval, the expedition was ready.

Ajo had chosen Jeditto as his botanist and Kaibab as his zoologist and pilot. Both were from the College of Cardinals. For his social anthropologist, he had chosen a young woman, Gisela, who had never participated on an expedition before. Being a newcomer, she was still being vetted by the Abbott's Committee and the window for launch time was quickly running.

Ajo, having been on several expeditions previously, knew the Committee liked to cut it close to launch when issuing approvals for new explorers. So he wasn't worried. At least not enough to share with anyone.

As he checked the departure for the umpteenth time, Ajo was less than pleasantly surprised when Father Naco confidentially strode the gantry way to the star cruiser. He struggled with a large duffle bag draped over one shoulder.

Father Naco was notorious for being a strict interpreter of the Church's laws and tenants. He would be doing all he could to discredit any findings found on the trip.

"Greetings my fellow travelers," Father Naco stated as he entered the cargo bay where Ajo and Tonalea were supervising the delivery of the last of the supplies.

"Father." Ajo replied, as Tonalea remained silent and bowed slightly. "I trust you are ready to begin our expedition."

"To find the Law Giver? Of course I am, though I doubt we'll find him in Orion's arm," he priest replied.

"That maybe so, but no one has ever looked there before," Ajo explained patiently. "There is a planet there that meets the requirements for advanced intelligent life and perhaps it holds the secret to the missing link to our culture. Even if it does not, we must confirm that it does not."

"Missing link?" Naco shouted, dismissing Ajo's statement. "Your statement borders heresy, Deacon." He dropped his duffle bag on the floor and took a defiant stance. "You academicians. You're all alike. You think you know the truth just because of some theory you devise to fit your half-baked ideas," the little priest practically spat out the words. "You need to remember the Church allows your College of Cardinals to exist as long as it continues to help provide a deeper meaning and understanding of the Church."

"And if the truth doesn't fit into the Church's archaic version of reality?" Ajo responded. "They are discarded."

The priest's voice dropped several octaves and took on a menacing tone. "As long as your research validates the Church's teachings you and your College of Cardinals are allowed to exist. You would be well served to remember that."

The priest then turned and started to walk away – then hesitated. "I have much to do before we leave, as I am sure you do. But as part of the Church's blessing for your expedition, you must attend a consecration ceremony this evening. Eight o'clock sharp." He turned to Tonalea. "Store my bag," he growled then left without another word or to wait for a response.

Once they were sure the priest was gone, Tonalea turned to Ajo and said, "Why do you antagonize him so? The expedition will be difficult enough without having him looking for anything he can use against you."

"I'm tired of the Church taking our scientific findings and twisting them to fit their dogma." Ajo complained, and then he yelled, "I'm tired of it!"

"What are you doing? He might hear you." Tonalea groused.

Ajo ignored her, turned to the group and said in a tone that was clearly contemptuous, "Let's finish up the preparations, then go to our *blessing*."

* * *

The expedition's star cruiser dropped out of light speed on the side of a desolate moon closest to a planet that orbits a red dwarf star. The planet's orbit is gravitationally locked to the star, like the moon's is to Earth. The result is a dayside of endless sunlight and a night side of darkness and packed ice. On the dayside, the planet was covered with water, with a scattering of small verdant islands floating in a dark blue sea.

"There!" cried Ajo, from the co-pilots seat. "There!" he stood pointing out the viewing port at the planet. Surrounding the entire planet from pole to pole was a crystal clear Ajo Sphere. It appeared to be in perfect condition and the ship's instruments were registering energy readings being generated by the sphere.

"Be sure to check for energy disbursement sources on each of the islands. The energy being generated by the sphere has to be dissipated in some way," Ajo instructed.

For the next hour, they circled the planet but found nothing until their instruments registered a change in the temperate zone of the northern hemisphere.

"Ajo, I believe I've found the disbursement source," Tonalea noted excitedly. "It is below us under that large mass of clouds off to our left at two o'clock."

"Let's take her down and investigate," Ajo ordered, and the Star Cruiser began descending through the cluster of clouds. When they broke through, there was a large lush green island with a strong energy reading directly below them.

With the Star Cruiser holding its altitude just below the cloud cover, expedition members boarded a shuttlecraft for the final descent to planet below. As they left the Cruiser Ajo called out to the team, "Remember where we parked."

As the shuttle descended, Ajo directed Kaibab to land off to their right in an open, grassy space. The rest of the island appeared to be covered with a dense primitive forest, rich with plant life.

"We need to measure the atmosphere before we open the shuttle," Tonalea the order and Jeditto began punching buttons on his console. "What are the readings?" Tonalea called out, clearly impatient.

"The atmosphere is dense," Jeditto replied. "Much denser than our world but tolerable."

"Alright then, grab the gear and let's go check this place out," Ajo instructed the crew.

"It hardly seems worth the trip. It's a dead planet," Father Naco remarked. "There isn't any advanced intelligent life here."

Ignoring the priest, Ajo called out last-minute instructions for the team. "Set your blasters on full. We don't know what we'll encounter. Double-check your explosives and ropes. Be sure everyone brings their picks, shovels and brooms. We'll probably need to do some excavating."

It was slow going as the team acclimated to the dense atmosphere. It didn't help they had to start hacking away at the grass as soon as the shuttle door was opened. What from the air appeared to be waist high grass was actually over six feet tall. Under the demand of carving out a path, it was kind of like trying to breathe while a garden hose was spraying you in the face.

"My arms feel like lead weights every time I lift my machete," Tonalea complained as she hacked at the undergrowth.

"Oh, I hear that, girl friend," Gisela carped between huffs and puffs of heavy breathing.

"It's absolutely beautiful," Tonalea gushed, still panting. "These plants are so strange looking and yet so beautiful."

"And would you just look at these trees. They're huge!" Kaibab pointed to a particularly gargantuan tree. "The meter says the big tree over there is more than half a mile tall and a hundred and forty feet around at the base. This is amazing."

Suddenly a pair of what appeared to be winged whales surged through the upper reaches of the trees, startling the team. They had to duck down, but the huge flying creatures paid them no notice as they pursued a swarm of what may have been insects, gulping in huge mouthfuls at a time. Their huge wings flapping in the heavy atmosphere buffeted the team, knocking them down to their knees as the heavy air flowed past them as if waves in an ocean on their home world. Before anyone could react and to document the creatures, they were gone merging with the forest once again.

"Did anyone get pictures of that?" Ajo cried out, but no one spoke up. "Great!" Ajo groused, and then continued forward, hacking away at the thick undergrowth.

Ajo suddenly stopped when he hacked an opening in the grass and discovered the trees had given way to a forest of large fern like vegetation. They were fan shaped with a large pointed stinger at the base of the huge leaves.

Jeditto could hardly control himself as he stumbled up next to Ajo. "Wow! Look at that!" He pushed past Ajo and began following what appeared to be an ambulatory root gliding into a maze of roots and leaves. "I've never seen or even heard of anything like this," he exclaimed as he disappeared into the maze. "I must gather some samples."

"Jeditto, don't..." Ajo started to yell, but he was cut off mid-sentence by a loud cry of anguish from within the maze. Gisela dropped her gear and, waving her machete wildly, charged into the maze of huge fauna.

"Jeditto," Gisela bellowed as she too disappeared into the maze of roots and stems.

"Wait, Gisela!" Ajo hollered, then swore loudly as she vanished before his eyes. "Damn it, people, you're supposed to follow my orders," Ajo screamed as he dropped his gear and ran after Gisela. His machete sliced through the maze as he raced after the two team members.

The others quickly followed, except for Father Naco who stood still patiently waiting for the others to emerge from the thick vegetation. There was no sense in all of them dying, as far as he was concerned.

Gisela reached Jeditto just as the root he was chasing began dragging him up to the center of the plant's leaves. The stinger had impaled Jeditto, incapacitating him so the plant could more easily feed.

Ajo arrived behind Gisela just in time to watch the plant swiftly lunging forward, its center stem splitting open to reveal a hellish multiple jawed mouth, one jaw set within the other in descending order. Each jaw was lined with a row of large spike like teeth. They watched in horror as the plant clamped down upon Jeditto's body piercing it and crushing it.

It was over before the others arrived, and Ajo and Gisela were already backing away from the plant.

"Where's Jeditto?" Tonalea asked as she tried to push past Ajo.

"Gone," Ajo stated curtly.

"What?" Tonalea questioned and tried to brush past Ajo. He grabbed her and held her back while pushing a crying Gisela towards Kaibab.

"No, it's too dangerous," Ajo stated firmly and dragged Tonalea back. "We have to get out of here. Now move it," Ajo barked and the remaining team members turned and began following the path back only to realize the path was quickly filling in behind them.

"I think we better run for it, the plants are growing in right behind us," Kaibab shouted, and the group started racing for the clearing.

They had almost escaped the maze when a root ensnared Kaibab's foot and knocked him down. He called out as he quickly spun himself around to hack at the root that was already trying to grab hold of his other foot.

Ajo turned and pulled his blaster from its holster and was about to fire when another blaster discharged its electrical load first, striking the root just inches beyond Kaibab's outstretched foot. The root splattered as the beam cut through it, releasing Kaibab's foot. There was a loud guttural groan as the root retreated into the maze.

Ajo quickly helped Kaibab to his feet, shaking in amazement. "I think we hurt it!"

"So much for making friends with our first contact," Kaibab quipped as Ajo helped him up. Together, the team managed to escape the maze, collapsing to the ground between the trees and the plants to catch their breath.

"I don't think it is a good idea to rest here. We need to be moving on quickly," Father Naco stated as he looked about in an effort to not be taken by surprise. Ajo looked up to see the space between the huge stems they had just hacked had already filled back in.

"Yes, yes, you are right, let's get going, double time," Ajo instructed the team as he grabbed his and Jeditto's gear.

As the team walked away briskly, Father Naco stood his ground against the approaching roots and said a brief prayer for Jeditto. Only then did he turn and walk away, quickly following the others.

* * *

The next two hours passed without incident, though the pace at which they were traveling was slow and deliberate. The vegetation was thick and difficult to cut, even with their machetes.

Shortly after taking over the lead to give Ajo a breather, Tonalea called out. "I think we're there. It's in a small valley just ahead of us."

"Really, what can you see?" Gisela asked.

Tonalea pointed to what looked like the remains of tall structures engulfed in plant growth. Vines encased what looked like the remains of concrete and steel buildings.

Father Naco pushed his way forward until he stood next to Tonalea and could see what she was seeing. "That's impossible," Father Naco shouted in disbelief.

"Believe it, Father," Tonalea informed him. "We're even standing on a paved surface."

"But the historic text says there is no world like our world. How is this possible?" Father Naco mumbled.

"That's what we're here to discover." Ajo informed him, smirking and barely concealing his glee.

"Run the energy scans. Let's try to pin point the source of the energy signature," Ajo instructed Tonalea, who quickly turned on her hand held scanner.

The deaconess scanned the area before them and said excitedly, "Yes. I'm getting a strong reading. There's an energy source in those ruins."

"Okay, we know our destination let's go!" Ajo ordered, and the team headed down the hillside towards the ruins below.

On the slope down, the undergrowth was considerably thinner, allowing the team to travel quickly to the bottom. On the valley floor the team made very good time crossing to the ruins.

"Where to now, Tonalea?" asked Ajo.

"The energy is emanating from the ruins of the structure in front of us."

"Let's find a way in," Ajo instructed.

After a diligent search of the building's perimeter, they found a cavity in the foundation where the roots of a massive tree had dislodged the concrete. One after the other, led by Ajo, the expedition entered the structure.

Following the beeping on Tonalea's scanner, they found themselves deep in the interior of the structure. In one of the many rooms, they found the power source.

"It's nuclear," Tonalea stated. "Probably a fusion battery. Primitive but an effective source of energy."

"We need to find a way up into the interior of this structure," Ajo noted.

After several minutes of searching, the team found a way up. It was a small vertical shaft that had a metal ladder running up the inside of it. To their initial dismay, the ladder had only gone as far as the next level, but once they had arrived there, they were pleasantly surprised.

The next level proved to be a large, open great hall. It was two stories tall with many back–illuminated skylights and several large pillars covered in dirt, grime and weeds.

"What do you think this place was?" asked Tonalea.

"A blasphemous place of worship," Father Naco chimed in. "We must leave here immediately. No God fearing ITL would remain in such a heretical place."

"How do you figure this a heretical place?" Ajo jumped on Father Naco's statement.

"Why, just look around you. There are pulpits everywhere and a giant cross there, above the alter." Father Naco pointed out.

"What? Are you mad? Those so called pulpits are kiosks. And the giant cross is merely damaged window frames," Ajo stated firmly while staring down Father Naco. "I'm in charge of this expedition and I'll give the orders, including when and if we leave certain areas. Now is that clear? It better be, because I will leave you here on this planet, if you continue." Ajo snarled at the priest. "Now, let's try and"

But Ajo's remark was cut short when a large beast burst into the structure.

The beast stood over five feet tall at its shoulders, with six legs, and was covered in what looked to be light green grass colored fur. Its face was ferocious. It had a shovel shaped jaw protruding outward like an alligator's jaw. Both the upper and lower jaws were covered with sharp spike shaped teeth.

After a momentary hesitation, the beast decided to attack the closest target, Father Naco.

The priest screamed with fright as the creature charged him.

Kaibab turned and raced towards Father Naco and at the last second, dove into the little priest, knocking him out of the way. Unfortunately by doing so, Kaibab himself was now in the center of the charging beast's line of attack.

As the beast plowed into Kaibab he tried to roll with the blow. He was sent several feet into the air and several yards off to the side. As he hit the ground, Kaibab let out a shriek and slid into a pile of rocks where he lay still.

Ajo, Tonalea and Gisela all fired their blasters within a second of each other. The women's blaster rounds bored into the beast's body, while Ajo's round struck the beast in the head.

The blaster had done the job, making short work of the marauding beast. Its final resting place was against one of the kiosks. The impact of the beast crashing into the kiosk had knocked the layers of dust and dirt built up over the ages, revealing the brightly colored six foot high monolith it had encrusted.

Father Naco and Gisela went to aid Kaibab and found he was bruised and battered but alive.

Ajo and Tonalea cautiously approached the beast to make sure it was dead. Upon confirming it was, they turned their attention to their injured team member.

"How's Kaibab?" Ajo asked with concern.

"Surprisingly well. He's battered and bruised but he's alive." Father Naco replied. "I believe if we can allow him a few minutes to regain his bearings, with a little help he can make it back to the shuttle."

"That's good news," Ajo responded and turned to talk to Tonalea but she wasn't there. She'd noticed the bright color on the kiosk and went to investigate.

Ajo walked over to where she was standing. "What have you found?"

"I'm not sure," she stated and pointed to the top of the kiosk.

Ajo followed her gaze and there, clear as day at the top of the kiosk, were the words, "Museum of Natural History."

It was in *their* language.

They looked at each other and quickly dug through their backpacks and pulled out rags and small knives to clear away the built up muck and grime.

Seeing what they were doing, Father Naco hollered as he approached them, "What are you doing? In the name of the Church of ITL - *stop that*! I command you to *stop*!" he bellowed as he plowed into Ajo, knocking him over while shoving Tonalea away from the kiosk. "You cannot view this blasphemy."

"What are you talking about? Have you lost your mind? Ajo shouted. "This is exactly why we made the expedition. This isn't absolute proof but it is some good evidence. Now back off before I use my blaster on you."

While the two men argued, Gisela helped Kaibab cross the space to the kiosk. They stopped on the side away from the ruckus.

"Hey, look here," Gisela noted, pointing to the side of the kiosk in front of her. "It looks like a picture of a humanoid.

"It's awfully hard to read. How can you be sure it says anything?" Father Naco stated as he looked over Tonalea's shoulder.

Ajo shoved past Father Naco to step up next to Gisela. He pointed towards another section of the kiosk. "Looks like a map. It seems to be directing us over there." And Ajo walked off across the great hall.

"Like I said, it's very hard to read. I would think it says it is this way," Father Naco pointed in the opposite direction of where Ajo was headed.

The rest of the team ignored him and continued following Ajo. After several seconds and a glance at the beast lying next to the kiosk, Father Naco quickly caught up with the others.

At the far side of the great hall, Ajo found a stairway that led up and without hesitation he began climbing. It was slow going due to the debris that covered the stairs and the fact that Kaibab had to be helped, but they managed to reach the second level and once there they stopped.

"Where to now?" Kaibab asked.

"See anything that looks like a kiosk or a humanoid?" Ajo asked.

"I'll look over this way," Gisela stated as she started to walk away.

"Be careful, have your blaster at the ready." Ajo instructed her. Then he turned to Tonalea and said. "Go with her and for God's sake be careful."

"See, I told you there wasn't anything here." Father Naco commented.

"Oh, do shut up!" Kaibab snapped at the priest. "If you don't stop being so negative, I'll feed you to the next beast we encounter."

"Right. Look at you. You can't even walk without help," Father Naco smirked at Kiabab.

"Yeah, but I can still shoot," he replied, catching the priest off guard.

Ajo turned back to Kaibab and said, "He's hardly worth the waste of energy. Does that tall tangle of weeds look like it could be a kiosk?" Ajo asked Kaibab, pointing at a tall clump of twisted vegetation.

"I'd be guessing, but I think so," Kaibab replied. "Give me a second and I'll scan it to be sure."

"Okay. Do that and while you're at it see if the scanner can pick up another set of stairs," Ajo added. "We can't get any higher on the ones we used to get here."

"Why is that?" Kaibab asked.

"They've collapsed."

"Okay, scanning." Kaibab stated and went to work.

Ajo had started to walk over to the weed-covered kiosk when Gisela called out. "Hey, we found something."

"We're on our way," Ajo called back, then turned to Father Naco and said, "Make yourself useful and help Kaibab."

"Hurry up!" Gisela yelled at the three men as they ambled across the large hall towards her. When they finally arrived, Ajo took one look and was less than impressed with what he saw.

"I don't see anything. It looks as though the roof is caved in. Where is Tonalea?" Ajo queried in quick succession.

"I'm back here," Tonalea called out, and Ajo could just barely see her through the debris. She was standing and staring at something that was hidden by the dense rubble.

It took Ajo a couple of minutes to climb over the debris to arrive at Tonalea's position. "What is so interesting that I'm risking life and limb to see?" Ajo asked as he glanced around.

"Over there by the collapsed wall, just a little to the right of that pile of garbage," Tonalea directed.

"Oh my God! Yes I see them!" Ajo was referring to the two humanoid figures standing in what the museum back on ITL would call a display. There was a fake tree in the display with the two figures. They were primitive men with sloping foreheads, long hair, beards and raised eye brows. They wore animal skins on their bodies for clothes. Their faces were forever held frozen, looking very aggressive.

Gradually, Ajo, Tonalea and Gisela made their way down the short incline to the display. Tonalea was documenting everything so it could be further studied when they returned home.

"Oh my God. This may just be the missing link!" Gisela shouted. "They are humanoid like us!"

Father Naco stepped to the edge of the debris slope with Kaibab and quickly assessed the situation. "Blasphemy!" he shouted. "Blasphemy against the Church of ITL and against ITL itself. These primitive beings cannot be our Law Givers. Burn it down! Destroy it!" Father Naco demanded.

"No!" Ajo cried out. "Let's think this over."

"Heretic!" Father Naco screamed at Ajo and pulled an explosive device from his backpack. As he swung it forward, he flipped the switch to arm it.

Ajo reacted immediately. He pulled his blaster and fired. The blast struck Father Naco in the side and spun him around.

Kaibab tried to grab him but he charged down the display with the bomb held high over his head.

"Take cover," Ajo screamed as he shoved the two women around and behind a debris pile.

A moment later, there was a fiery blast that incinerated the two humanoid figures and most of the display area.

When the survivors dared to peek out from behind their protective piles of rubble, there was nothing left to see.

No display and no Father Naco.

"Damn it!" Cried Tonalea. "That crazy priest tried to kill us and destroyed our evidence." Turning to Ajo she cried, "What do we do now?"

Ajo did not immediately respond. Like the others, he was in shock at the furiousness of the attack. After a minute or so he finally spoke, "The Priest was crazy but he might have been right."

"Now you're sounding crazy," Kaibab stated.

Ajo walked over to the remains where the humanoids had stood. He looked down and said, "Sophisticated beings like us could not have sprung from such primitive beings as these."

"But if these were not our missing link," Tonalea began to say, "then…"

Ajo raised his hand to cut her off. Something caught his attention. He continued to walk around the debris field caused by the explosion until he suddenly stopped and pointed down at something in the remains.

"Come here and look at this." He pointed to a room that was now exposed through a hole in the floor. "We need to go back downstairs."

The four remaining team members returned to the lower level and searched for the room beneath the explosion area and after a short time found it. Above the doorway leading into the room was a sign that read *'Age of Technology'*.

They wandered around tables of strange objects when Ajo stopped at one. It was a shiny flat clamshell devise. He examined it and saw that he could lift the cover up. He opened the ancient device to inspect it and saw many small buttons on one side and a broken glass display screen on the other.

"What did you find?" asked Tonalea.

"I don't know," Ajo replied.

"What's that?" Tonalea asked, pointing to a grime covered label on the device, then said in shock. "It's has the letters I-T-L on it. The letters of our Church!"

Ajo placed his fingers on the label and began to scrap off the grime, revealing all the words on the ancient laptop computer.

It read *'INTEL Inside'*.

THE ORACLE

ONE MAN'S SCIENCE IS ANOTHER MAN'S RELIGION

Three hundred thousand years ago - before the dawn of civilization - Tacna, younger brother of Jano and son to the chief of his clan, Paiute walked through a harsh land of the Ice Age, searching for game or any kind of sustenance in the stark, hard landscape.

Tacna was small for a Cro-Magnon. Much smaller than his brother Jano – in fact, smallest for his clan - a fact that awarded him little status, although he was one of the chief's sons.

Today he was searching a marshland. It was a stark landscape, and game was scarce. A seasoned lone hunter, Tacna was well aware of the dangers a single hunter faced in the wilds. He was constantly on guard for predators stalking him. Always looking around, he was alert for unknown threats and dangers.

One danger was always present.

Neanderthals.

As an early Cro-Magnon man, his species was constantly in competition, and sometimes in conflict, with the Neanderthals over food and territory. Just the thought made him cling his stone-tipped spear tighter in his hand.

He was stalking what he believed was a wounded mammoth when he heard a strange sound. It was a mournful sound, leading him to believe he was close to an easy kill. The thought of bringing back such a trophy pleased Tacna and as he neared a large rock fall, he readied his spear for the kill.

Suddenly, the sound changed. It morphed into a strange hum he had never heard before and it was growing louder and louder as though it was coming towards him. He looked up and saw a bright shiny object fly over the top of the craggy trees a short distance away.

In an instant, it was gone.

It had dropped down into the trees some distance off with a deafening roar that hurt Tacna's ears. He ducked behind a pile of large stones to try to shield himself from the strange flying creature that roared so loud.

Tacna stayed behind the rock pile for several minutes, though time beyond day and night meant little to him. When he felt the beast would have passed, he slowly ventured a peek around the edge of the rocks. He could see nothing but a strange yellow glow back among the trees.

The glow was coming from well within Neanderthal territory, and he was rightfully afraid of venturing there alone. The Neanderthals were fierce warriors and easily twice Tacna's size. If a Neanderthal caught him they would kill him. But the glow seemed to call to him. Finally, Tacna could not help himself, he had to know and so, he scampered across the rocky field into the woods.

Entering the thick woods, Tacna could see the glow was off to his right and there was smoke hanging in the limbs of bare trees. As he closed on the glow, he saw a second red glow in the distance, this one from a fire on the ground. Its smoke plume rose straight up through the trees into the clear blue cloudless sky above. That had to be Neanderthals.

Following the smoke, Tacna found himself standing on the edge of an open space among the trees. The shiny creature that had flown passed him was now sitting next to a fast-moving stream. Tacna knew the stream led to a river and then to a vast sea filled with vicious beasts. The bright shiny creature had just three legs. They were thin and shiny with large round paws. Tacna had never seen a creature so large and round outside of the sea turtles they hunted in the spring when they mated on the edge of the vast sea.

He was about to approach the creature when suddenly its side opened up, making a hissing sound much like a snake, only much louder, and a smaller creature emerged from inside. Tacna, now frightened, quickly darted behind a nearby tree and tried to prepare himself to fight for his life against this strange figure.

Several seconds passed as Tacna hid in fear but once again his curiosity got the better of him, so he peeked around the tree.

The figure was certainly not a Neanderthal. This creature was tall and thin with long sinewy arms and legs and its skin was silvery like the creature it had climbed out of. Its head was elongated and its eyes were set deep in their sockets. It moved in a slow, deliberate manner, as if it wasn't used to walking. It made several circles around the larger creature before it seemed to be able to move with more ease.

As Tacna watched, the strange figure reached over its shoulder and pulled a shiny stone from a pack on his back. It then waved it around. When it pointed the shiny object at Tacna's hiding place, he slumped behind a tree.

Suddenly, the strange figure took two steps toward Tacna who tried to make himself even less visible behind the tree, readying to attack the strange figure. But the creature stopped walking towards Tacna and instead had turned away. When Tacna peeked again, the creature was walking up the stream bank away from him.

The little Cro-Magnon followed the strange creature, keeping a good distance behind it but within eyesight. The creature walked a short distance to a cave hidden in a boulder field at the bottom of a tall cliff over which the stream cascaded in a waterfall.

Upon entering the cave, the strange figure took off his pack and set it on the ground. He opened it and spread out several items from his pack, then kneeled down next to the items on the floor of the cave.

Tacna watched from behind a boulder at the mouth of the cave. He peeked now and then, trying to see exactly what this strange figure was doing, but it was too dark in the cave to see clearly. Through the dim light, Tacna did see that the strange figure had another shiny object. Tacna was once again overwhelmed by curiosity. He could see the creature twisting one end of a silvery log - how could he do that?

Suddenly, the object threw a bright light up towards the cave's ceiling and the whole cave became as bright as day.

Tacna was overwhelmed with awe now and stepped closer. He'd stepped several feet from his hiding place when the creature turned and looked straight at him. Tacna froze for a moment and then on wobbly legs turned to run away, but tripped over an exposed root and fell face first to the ground.

Even before Tacna could scramble to his feet, which was quite fast, something grabbed his arm and pulled him up. To his horror, Tacna found he was face to face with the strange creature.

"Are you alright?" The strange creature asked in Tacna's own tongue. Tacna's stare prompted the creature to ask him, "Are you injured?"

Tacna was unable to speak as he looked into those deep-set eyes, so he just shook his head, 'no'. Tacna now understood this was a man and not a creature, and his fear level dropped several notches, though he was still ill at ease.

"Come, we'll get warm by the fire," the stranger said as he walked over to where there had been a fire pit in the center of the cave. The stranger motioned for Tacna to sit on a large rock and he complied, though he watched the stranger very closely, with his mouth agape and his eyes locked in a frightened stare.

The stranger's clothes were not made of animal skins as Tacna's were. His clothes were shiny and covered him all over except his head and hands. As he stood at the mouth of the cave, the wind caused it to flutter and Tacna felt the chill of the wind. He looked to the sky and saw the heavy dark clouds building to the west. Those clouds would bring rain and being close to a fire would be a good thing, Tacna thought, as it always grew colder when it rained.

"I am Supai," the stranger said in a calm voice while extending his hand to Tacna. "And you are?"

Tacna hesitated a few moments. He was wondering how this stranger knew the language of his clan. The stranger waited for Tacna's response and finally he spoke.

"You are a Supai?" he asked, wondering if that was the stranger's clan.

"Oh no," the stranger corrected him. "My *name* is Supai. I am from a race of people called the 'Preez'.

Tacna nodded slowly then said, "I am Tacna. I am second son of the chief of our clan."

"Good to meet you, Tacna. Is your clan cave far from here?"

"No, not too far, but not too close, this is Neanderthal territory."

"Oh, I see. If this is not your territory, then why are you here?" Supai asked. "Are you not afraid?"

"I am careful. I saw the shiny bird and followed."

"That's good." Supai stated.

"Why you here?" Tacna asked.

"I'm here to help you."

"Help me?"

"Help you and your people. That is what my people do, we help people," the Preez shared.

"How?" Tacna asked. He was no longer feeling threatened, his natural curiosity was surfacing again.

"I can give your people the gift of fire." Supai stated.

"We have fire." Our Fire Master guards the flame we harvested from a burning tree long ago. A great streak of light came from the sky and struck the tree, setting it on fire." Tacna shared.

"But can you *make* fire?" The stranger winked at Tacna.

"Only the great streak of light from sky can make fire," Tacna assured the stranger.

"What would you say if I said I could make fire, right here and right now?" Supai pointed to the fire pit.

"Make fire? How?" Tacna asked, a questioning look on his face.

"I'll show you," The Preez stated.

Supai crouched down next to the fire pit and pulled two small rocks from his pants pocket, which in itself caused Tacna to look at his pants with curiosity. He even reached out and touched the slit that formed the opening for the pocket.

"We call that a pocket." Supai stated, then returned to his fire making.

"Pocklock," Tacna tried to say the strange word.

"Pocket," the Preez repeated.

"Pokit," Tacna tried again.

Supai turned from the fire pit and looked right at Tacna and said the word slowly once more, "Pocket."

Tacna watched and listened closely, then gave it a moment of thought before blurting out, "Pocket."

"Very good, Tacna, very good," Supai congratulated the little Cro-Magnon.

"Pocket." Tacna repeated the word over and over several times before he was quiet again.

"Now, shall we get started making our fire?" Supai asked. He then opened his pack and pulled out some small pieces of wood and a handful of dried grass. Supai set the pieces of wood down on the ground. The grass he placed in, under and around the wood. He then began clicking the two stones together. At first, nothing happened.

"I see no fire." Tacna stated.

The Preez ignored Tacna's comment and continued clicking the two stones together. When Tacna looked closer at what Supai was doing, he saw little white sparks jumping off the two stones and landing in the dried grass. After several sparks landed in the grass, a whiff of smoke appeared on the dried grass. Supai gently waved his hand near the smoldering grass and, after a few seconds, a flame burst forth.

The flames from the burning grass caused the small pieces of wood to start burning, which pleased Supai very much. As he added several pieces of kindling wood to the fire, he thought about how easy fire was created on his world. They had lighters, initiators, and accelerants. To have fire on his home planet, it took as little as a flip of the switch. It was a trivial thing. Here it took a practiced skill, and it was a matter of life and death.

The making of fire astounded Tacna. He quickly grabbed two random stones off the floor of the cave and started smashing them together, but there was no spark. He turned to the Preez, with a look of utter befuddlement on his face.

"It doesn't work with just any stone," he said. "It has to be a stone like these, flint. There is lots of flint along the river and out among the rocks outside the forest." Supai held up the two stones so that Tacna could see the difference between the rocks he held and those that the Preez had used. He held them out for Tacna to try making sparks with them.

He clicked them together hard, but there was no spark. "What kind of magic stone are these?" Tacna asked, as he continued to bang them together.

"Here, let me show you again," Supai stated and took the stones from Tacna. He showed how he struck the stones together. He did this slowly so Tacna could see how the stones barely met and then scraped together, producing a spark. He then handed back the sparking stones to Tacna, and he promptly began practicing striking the stones with a glancing blow and soon he too was making the stones spark.

The Preez smiled as he watched Tacna gleefully strike the stones together time after time, again and again. Finally, he grabbed Tacna's hands, stopping him. He then made a pile of grass and small pieces of wood, making sure Tacna understood that the grass had to be all around the small pieces of wood. He then nodded for Tacna to strike the stones together and when it sparked, the dried grass started to burn and a moment after that, the small pieces of wood started to burn as well.

Tacna began gleefully jumping for joy. He knew what this meant. The clan would accept him and show great respect, for he alone knew how to make fire. He alone would be called, "Fire Starter."

* * *

Tacna spent the rest of the day practicing his new skill. When the sun began to hide itself, he said his goodbyes to the Preez and ran most of the way back to his clan, arriving just after dark.

The clan was gathered to eat the day's kill. His father, Paiute and his brother Jano were sitting where they always sat, on one side of the fire with the rest of the clan on the other side. Paiute and Jano were dividing up the meat between the clan members based on their perceived value to the clan.

Tacna strode into the cave, bypassing the place off to the side where he usually sat. He walked instead right up to his father and brother and sat down right in front of them.

"What it this? You cannot sit here," Jano growled. "You are weak and you are being disrespectful. Go sit over there where you belong," he ordered.

Tacna said nothing, but did not move either. Instead, he pulled dried grass and small twigs from inside his tunic and piled them just as the Preez had done. He then began scraping the two stones together. He was nervous, and he failed to do it properly for several minutes, but then he settled down and found the right angle. Small sparks began showering the dried grass. Every member of the clan sat staring at Tacna, watching intently, except Jano.

"Enough of this foolishness. Go take your place." Jano roared, but Paiute raised his hand to silence him, for he was curious.

Jano sat fuming with jealousy because his inferior brother was the center of attention. After another minute, he could no longer control himself. Jano stood up, stepped towards Tacna and was about to kick the pile of grass and twigs away when a flame erupted from the pile. Jano jumped back in surprise. The rest of the clan gasped in awe and began mumbling excitedly.

Tacna proceeded to stoke the small flame with his breath until the sparked flames had grown into a small fire.

"Magic!" exclaimed Paiute. Many of the clan repeated his utterance and muttered excitedly among themselves, except Jano.

Jano cried out loudly, "It's a trick!"

"No!" the Chief shouted. "Tacna is to be praised. We no longer have to worry our fire may go out."

Jano turned to Tacna and spat at him, "Teach us this magic," he demanded.

Tacna stared up at his hated older brother for the longest time, then said, "I can't. Only I can command the fire." He then tucked the flints back inside his tunic, jumped up and ran off into a rainy night.

* * *

A few hours later, he was at the Preez cave.

"Did you show your people the gift of fire?" asked Supai.

Tacna smiled and nodded. "Teach me more so I can help my clan."

The Preez taught Tacna many things over the next few days that would help feed and help cure the clan members of illness or help heal their wounds. On the fifth day, the Preez built a large fire and half covered it with a strange-looking pile of stones.

The stones were piled up in nearly a full circle around the fire. They were stacked several stones high and at the top was a large flat stone with a circle of smaller stones on top of it. Inside the circle of smaller stones, Supai packed clay and inside the clay he dropped a few pieces of a strange reddish stone that he had picked up in the back of the cave.

The Preez then took several tree branches and tied them together, making a near solid grouping. He then handed it to Tacna explaining he was to fan the flames of the fire while Supai added more wood.

Tacna did as he was instructed and slowly the reddish rock began to glow and melt. It was melting just like ice does in spring or when you set it next to the fire. Out of curiosity, Tacna reached out as if to touch the melting rock. Supai grabbed his arm roughly and pulled it back.

"Do *not* touch! Hot! Do you understand hot?" Supai asked.

Tacna just stared at him, clearly not comprehending.

Supai then grabbed a large stick and told Tacna to watch. Supai jabbed the stick into the semi molten rock. A flame immediately began to burn on the end of the stick.

He held it out to Tacna, who backed away from it, muttering, "Fire hot. Hurts."

"Fire hurt, yes." Supai repeated, pleased that Tacna understood that it would hurt him if he touched it. "Fire, no touch." He said, making sure Tacna understood.

The Preez instructed Tacna to keep fanning the flame as he added more rock on top and more wood to the fire.

An hour passed, and the Preez used two sticks that he had soaking in water to pick up the semi molten rock. He took the gooey glob over to a large flat rock and he dropped it on top of it. He used one stick, holding it in his left hand to hold the goo in place, and took a rock in his right hand and began pounding the red-hot goo with it.

Tacna watched as Supai hit the glowing red rock again and again until it was flat. He then beat on it some more until it looked like a long spear point. It took several hours to get it just right, but once it was done Supai smiled at his craftsmanship.

Then, using the two wet sticks, he picked up the still hot spear point and placed it first in the water where it made a loud hissing sound like a snake. Then continuing to use the sticks, he took the spear point and set it against the wall of the cave. He repeated the process to make a smaller spear point that he also set aside, as he had the big spear point.

All through the night, Tacna lay staring at the long spear point. Try as he might, he could not comprehend its purpose.

When morning came, Tacna could barely control his excitement. Supai picked up the long spear point in his hands, stepped over to a boulder and began banging the spear point on it, hard.

Each blow made a loud ringing sound. Chips of stone flew off in all directions. When he was sure the long spear point was solid and wasn't going to break in use, he stopped and told Tacna to get his spear.

"Now attack me, Tacna. Attack me. It's okay." Supai directed him.

Tacna just stood there staring at him. He wasn't going to attack his teacher.

Seeing Tacna's hesitation, Supai decided to try a different approach.

"Tacna, does this interest you?" Supai asked as he held up the long spear point.

Tacna nodded vigorously. "Then I need you to get your spear and attack me, so I can show you how it works."

Tacna retrieved his spear and he lined up across from Supai holding his spear with both hands as he prepared to jab at Supai.

"Ready?" Supai asked.

Tacna nodded and lunged at Supai. To Tacna's surprise, Supai used the long spear point to block Tacna's lunges.

The Preez smoothly stepped to the side as Tacna lunged again. By moving to the side as he did, Tacna missed Supai and was now standing very close to him. With one swift swing of the long spear point, Supai brought it down on top of Tacna's spear shaft, slicing it in two. Then he swiftly swung the long spear point upward until it was right under Tacna's chin.

Tacna stood there, his eyes full of fright.

Supai smiled at Tacna and said, "See how it works? It's called a sword. With it you can cut a small animal's head off as easily as I cut your spear in half. You can use a sword to slice, stab, throw or chop. Your spear requires you to jab at your enemy and that takes time. You have to lean in and then lean back - pushing out and pulling back".

He continued. "The sword can be swung back and forth easily and quickly, so you can move fast. Here, hold this," Supai handed Tacna the sword, "while I get you a target to stab and chop."

Tacna spent the day practicing with the sword and, as night fell, he stopped and said to Supai. "With this sword I can kill a Mammoth with one thrust."

"Yes," replied Supai. "With more bronze weapons your clan will quickly become dominant and your hunters will all be more successful while hunting. Animals will fall at your feet."

"And so will my enemies," Tacna thought.

* * *

Early the next morning, eager to try out the new weapon, Tacna took the sword and went hunting. A few hours into the hunt, he hadn't seen or heard a single animal. He was about to give up when he spotted a mature Wooly Bison resting in a clump of short twisted trees.

Tacna began a slow stalk of the bison. When he had crept close enough to throw his spear, he threw it and it struck the beast in its side right where the beast's heart should be. It impaled deeply into the beast and lodged there. The beast managed just two steps before it collapsed to the ground.

Tacna thought it was a good throw. Supai had made it to replace the spear he had cut in half. It had the new melted rock for a spear tip and the shaft was made of something he didn't understand, but it was hard and cold. It was also extremely easy to throw and flew straight and sure as the Preez had promised.

As Tacna approached the beast, it suddenly stirred and managed to get to its feet. Tacna backed up slowly as the beast stumbled towards him. He drew the sword Supai had made and held it exactly the same way that Supai had shown him.

Despite his fear, he stood his ground, believing he was a much better hunter with the sword.

When the beast lunged at him, Tacna followed the simple instructions of Supai.

He sidestepped the lunging beast.

As it stumbled past him, Tacna swung the sword down with all his might and chopped a large gash in the beast's neck. Blood spurted from the animal's neck, spraying Tacna in the face as well as all over his tunic.

The bison dropped to the ground and died a few minutes later. Tacna danced, for he had killed a bison and the clan would have to accept him as a warrior now.

He cut off the horns of the beast as proof of his great kill. With these horns, he would be considered every bit a man as his older brother Jano.

As he began tying the horns together so he might drag them back as proof of his deed, a sound that Tacna was very familiar with pierced the quiet day's solitude. It was a war cry. The war cry of his Clan. He dropped his prize and ran towards the sound of the skirmish.

* * *

Back at the cave, the Preez awoke. He noted that Tacna was gone and decided to see how he taught his clan the new knowledge bestowed upon him. As he walked towards what he believed was Tacna's village, he heard the sounds of conflict.

* * *

Tacna raced through the woods and out onto the frozen tundra. In the distance, he could hear the sound of the battle raging. He ran as fast as he could up a hill on the path to his clan's cave and, as he crested the hill, he found himself overlooking the battle.

Down below, Jano and the clan's warriors were fighting a large group of Neanderthals over a dead mammoth. Whose kill it actually was, was not the issue. The clan needed the meat. It was a matter of survival.

Without hesitation, Tacna raised his new bronze sword and charged down the hill, screaming at the top of his lungs.

His scream drew the attention of a large Neanderthal warrior who quickly turned to confront him. The Neanderthal raised his hard wooden club and swung it at Tacna.

Tacna, in turn, swung the sword at the Neanderthals club, striking it solidly and breaking it off just above where the Neanderthal gripped it.

Stunned, the Neanderthal stood there, his mouth agape, as he stared at the broken piece of the club in his hand.

Before he could react, Tacna was swinging the sword again. This time the sword struck his Neanderthal in the neck, slicing through it with the same ease that Tacna had sliced off the bison's horns. Another Neanderthal charged Tacna. The little Cro-Magnon lunged at him and thrust his sword forward, impaling the Neanderthal through his heart.

Seeing two members of their clan die so quickly and easily at the hand of this new warrior, the Neanderthals broke off their attack and fled.

Jano, who saw Tacna kill the two Neanderthals, walked over to him and stared at the strange weapon. "Give that to me." he ordered. "Only a warrior should have such a powerful weapon and I am the chosen leader after father dies.”

“No!” Tacna shouted. “I am the most powerful warrior in the clan and that makes me the true leader of the clan now.”

“You brazen little worm,” Jano shouted as he rushed forward, trying to grab the sword from Tacna.

Tacna stepped to the side, dodging Jano just as he had the bison. Then just as he had done with the bison, as Jano stumbled past he swung sword down upon his neck. The blow was clean and fast, slicing right through Jano, beheading him. Jano fell to the ground, his head rolling several feet away.

Tacna stared at his brother's body for a moment and then, hearing grumbling among the warriors of the clan, he quickly spun around to face them. He raised his sword and asked if anyone wanted to challenge his leadership, but they instantly quieted down, diverting their eyes. No one challenged him.

Tacna sneered at them and then turned away, walking off in the direction of the Preez cave.

He hadn't noticed Supai squatting in a clump of brush a few yards away. He was unaware that Supai had seen the whole battle - had seen him kill his brother.

* * *

Tacna, giddy with excitement, returned to Supai's cave, anxious to learn more Preez secrets. When he arrived, Supai confronted him.

"You used my weapon to kill your brother!" Supai screamed at him. "You lied to me. You told me you would teach your clan, not try to use what I've taught you to rule over them."

Tacna was speechless. He feared what the obviously smarter Supai would do. He cowered in the corner. "What are you going to do to me? Will you harm me?" Tacna anxiously asked.

"No, it is not our way. I will do more than harm you. I will go to your chief and tell him who I am and that I am here to teach his entire clan my secrets." Supai frowned at Tacna. "You will lose the power you have wrongly usurped. Your clan will cast you out for having plotted to control them." Supai turned away and started to head out of the cave.

Tacna's fear quickly turned to anger. He drew the sword and raced up behind Supai and drove the sword deep into Supai's back.

The Preez cried out in pain and fell to the ground. Looking up at Tacna, Supai saw the blood lust in his eyes. "No, please no," Supai pleaded, as Tacna raised the sword over his head. "Please, no," were the last words the Preez would say.

His pleading fell on deaf ears. Tacna swung the sword. It sliced fatally through Supai's neck, just as it had the bison, the two Neanderthals and Jano. A strange colored fluid ran down Supai's torso and bubbled from his nose and mouth as he gasped his last breath.

Tacna stood staring down at his handy work for several minutes, then grabbed Supai's pack of secrets and left the cave.

* * *

It was nightfall when Tacna arrived at the cave of his clan.

Chief Paiute and the others were speaking loudly. Though he couldn't hear them clearly, the tone was one of worry and fear. Stepping further into the cave, the conversation became clear. The clan was discussing the battle with the Neanderthal, Tacna and his new weapon. When they saw Tacna emerge out of the darkness, they all fell silent.

Tacna confidently and boldly walked up to the campfire and raised Supai's pack high into the air. "I will share my secrets with the clan if you accept me as your leader." He looked directly at Paiute.

Paiute stood up and bowed his head in acceptance. "Tell us what we should call you, Oh Powerful One."

The little Cro-Magnon, feeling his great power and influence in his clan, thought back to the Preez body lying on the cold cave floor.

After a moment's thought, he said, "Call me - Priest."

REVENGE

An ailing Adolf Hitler poured over a map of imaginary German armies, moving the now defunct units around the map with an uncontrollable palsy trembling hand covered in sallow skin. But in reality, what was left of Berlin was defended by old men and teenagers hurriedly conscripted from the Hitler Youth.

He squinted through filmed over eyes, sunken now in sockets on a puffy face--his head sunk into his shoulders. He only nibbled at his vegetarian meal of mashed potatoes and thin vegetable broth. The once vibrant Fuhrer, who captivated millions with his charismatic fiery speeches that cast a spell over the crowds, now was a sickly, bitter and premature old man.

His present life now consisted of sullen days and enraged nights in the thirty room Fuhrerbunker twenty-eight feet below the gardens of the Chancellery. The bunker was crowded and oppressive and the air was foul. Russian artillery units were constantly shelling what remained of the Chancellery building above it.

The mood in the bunker over the last few weeks would swing wildly from one extreme to another. There would be a temporary explosion of hope and then confidence would collapse again.

The main topic of conversation now was suicide and whether Hitler's entourage of civil servants and Army officers should take cyanide pills or shoot themselves in the head when the Russians arrived. Many who wished to live had secretly stored civilian clothes in order to change into them and try to escape when the opportunity presented itself.

In strategy sessions that ran to four in the morning, the half-crazed Fuhrer of Germany issued wild orders, refusing to accept that the German army was defeated. Few if any of his orders had been sent out. Most were addressed to commanders of army divisions that no longer existed or to generals he had ordered executed months ago. Hitler, now sullen and defeated, was determined to bring down the Reich capital with him in a personal Gotterdammerung.

He would rant, "Everyone has lied to me. Everyone has deceived me. No one has told me the truth. The generals have lied to me. The German people have not fought heroically. They deserve to perish. It is not *I* who have lost the war, but the German people".

Under this gloomy cloud, Hitler ordered his staff to prepare for the end and Hitler's SS bodyguards were ordered to destroy his personal papers.

After one of the last late night ranting strategy sessions, Hitler called his personal valet, Heinz Linge, to his private quarters. In less than 24 hours, the Russian Army will enter Hitler's underground bunker and the Fuhrer's dream of world conquest through National Socialism will be dead.

He placed a quivering hand on the young man's shoulder and, remembering the gruesome photos of Mussolini and his mistress stripped naked and strung up in the Piazza Loreto in Milan for public abuse, said, "You must never allow my corpse to fall into the hands of the Russians. They would make a spectacle in Moscow out of my body and put it in a waxworks."

But Linge replied, "Mein Fuhrer. You need not die here."

Hitler shook his head. "There is no escape from my fate." He picked up a dispatch lying on his desk. "Russian tanks are only 300 meters away from the Chancellery. I cannot take the chance of leaving this bunker and be captured by the Russians." He hung his head. "No. I will die here." He looked up and stiffened. "And you will carry out my last order."

That order was for the bodies of Hitler and his soon to be wife, Eva Braun, to burned after their suicide.

"Mein Fuhrer," Linge replied. "May I escort someone from the Special Weapons Unit to see you?"

Hitler shook his head. "It's too late for that. Whatever scientific miracles we had capable of defeating our enemies – that time has come and past."

But Linge would not relent. "Just a few moments of your time, Mein Fuhrer. Just a few moments—for your loyal servant."

Hitler gave a bleary-eyed stare at his longtime aide then said, "Alright, Linge. For you, a few moments."

The tall stately valet hurried from the room as Hitler opened a drawer on the right-hand side of his desk and pulled out a copy of his book 'Mein Kampf' – *My Struggle*. He fingered through the pages, then tossed it aside. He reached back into the drawer again and drew out a crumpled picture of his nemesis, Winston Churchill. He glared at the photo, then dropped it in front of him and cupped his face in his hands.

He must have dosed off because he was startled by a knock on the door.

Without waiting for the Fuhrer to give him permission to enter, Linge stepped through the door pulling along behind him a nearly bald, pasty white, bi-speckled old man who, upon entering the room, shouted, "Heil Hitler".

Hitler glanced at the old man and then at Linge. The Fuhrer did not return the salute. "Linge, you're bringing me an old man? Fine get on with it." Hitler sagged in his chair as he crumpled the photograph of Churchill for the last time before shoving it back into the drawer.

"This is Professor Gadsden," Linge announced and then nodded to the professor.

"Mien Fuhrer," Professor Gadsden replied. "I can save you from the Russians. I can save you from all of the Allies."

Hitler sighed heavily, "There is no saving me from my fate, Professor. There is nowhere I can hide. I cannot escape Berlin at this late date even if I dared."

"Perhaps there is no place but a time," the Professor said cryptically.

A look of confusion crossed Hitler's face as he asked, "Place? Time? I don't understand. You need to explain it clearly to me, Professor. Mind you, I am not in mood for scientific claptrap."

"Allow me to explain, Mien Fuhrer," the old Professor stated with a gleam in his eye. "As you know, the allies have overrun our research labs but we were able to smuggle out - just prior to their arrival - enough plutonium for the machine."

"The machine?" Hitler asked, "What machine?"

"A temporal apparatus," the old Professor stated in a quiet voice.

"A what?" Hitler groused.

"A time machine, Mien Fuhrer. A time machine."

Hitler gave Linge a stern look and then stared menacingly at the old professor. "I'm not in the mood for your nonsense, Professor. A time machine? Ha!" Hitler barked. "Linge, tell me why I should not send you and this charlatan out to defend the city!"

"Mien Fuhrer, it is true the machine does exist - and it works!" Linge quickly responded.

"It does, does it? Where is this machine?" Hitler demanded.

"It's in one of the ante rooms a few levels down." Gadsden blurted out. His eyes had lit up at the possibility of showing the Fuhrer his invention. "It can transport you to another time. You can go back to before the war and correct the mistakes that were made. You could have a second chance at winning the war against Roosevelt and Churchill." The Professor sounded very convincing.

Hitler sat silent for a moment, thinking, then said, "Yes, I could win the war if I knew what was to happen before it happened. I could defeat that bastard Churchill. He alone is the one man most responsible for my defeat." Hitler glanced at Linge, then at the old professor, "Take me to the machine," he ordered.

Linge, with the professor in tow, led the Fuhrer into the bowels of the fuhrerbunker. They had to traverse several ladders, iron stairways and pass through several steel bulkheads until finally they arrived at a heavy metal entry door. It took the old professor several tries to find the right key, but he managed to get them into the chamber and lock the door behind them.

The chamber was empty.

"I see nothing here," Hitler snarled at Linge.

"We have one more door before we are at the lab," Linge assured the Fuhrer.

They crossed the large chamber to what appeared to be a pile of rubble from across the room, but up close, it was merely a painting hung on rollers that slid to the side to expose the doorway behind it.

"What is this?" Hitler asked.

"Camouflage," Linge retorted as he shoved the painting out of the way.

The Professor once again nervously fumbled to try to find the right key to unlock the door, but finally the trio stepped into the lab.

There, in the center of the room, sat a huge contraption that consisted of two large semi-conical Plexiglas spheres – the kind of material fighter plane cockpits were made of. The spheres were separated by about a meter and a half. In between was a seat and what looked like a console from one of their jet powered planes. The console was on a hydraulic arm attached to the ceiling.

The trio walked across the large chamber to the machine and as the Fuhrer stood staring at it, the old professor flipped a switch behind him.

Hitler was about to touch one of the levers when the professor called out, "Please, do not touch the machine just yet."

Hitler pulled his hand back and gave the professor a nasty look but he wasn't paying attention. He was busy turning dials and flipping switches. Right away a hum filled the room, not so loud as to interfere with talking, but loud enough to be noticed.

The Fuhrer looked at Linge, who nodded reassuringly. "How does it work?" he asked.

"It is relatively simple," the old professor began chattering with wild enthusiasm. His pride in his accomplishment was all too obvious. "This stick controls the direction of time." The Professor pointed at a metal pole with a handgrip on its top that penetrated the floor next to the seat. "Push it forward and you go into the future. Pull it back and you go into the past." He pointed to the display panel in front of the chair. "And these knobs send you to a place and time" he stated as he started turning them, scrolling through a list of places and dates until the display read, Berlin, 1932.

"There," the Professor said. "You can relive your Reich and make the world safe for National Socialism."

But Hitler was hearing none of his chatter. His mind, now engrossed in one thought - *kill* Winston Churchill.

Should he kill his nemesis, he would have the sweetest of revenge. The one man standing between him and world domination would be no more. He reached out and grabbed the knob on the console and spun the knob until it read London, 1932.

Before Gadsden or Linge could react, Hitler leaped into the seat on the machine just as the two Plexiglas spheres began to rotate rapidly around the seat and console. Immediately Hitler grabbed the stick and pulled it back.

"No!" shouted the Professor. Linge tried to time the spacing between the rotating spheres but was unable to do so. Twice his arms were banged out of the way by the passing sphere.

The Professor and Linge watched in awe as the spheres rotated faster and faster until they were a blur. The seat bounced vigorously up and down while rocking sideways. Hitler clung to the arms on the seat for dear life. His face was a mask of fear.

A few seconds after the spheres blurred, there was a bright flash of light. The machine was gone along with its occupant.

* * *

The physical shock of the transport had momentarily disorientated Hitler. He had lost consciousness, and it took several seconds to regain his balance and realize he wasn't lying on a floor but leaning against a wall.

Glancing around, he saw the machine a few feet away. The machine smoldered as if it had been on fire, but there were no charred surfaces, no flames, and no heat emanating from the machine. He held his hand out in its direction and instead of hot, it felt chillingly cold.

The space around him was shrouded in darkness, and it took several seconds for his eyes to adjust.

He was in a room, a bedroom, from the look of it. A bed, nightstands, dresser and a couple of winged backed easy chairs sat by a fireplace, though there was no fire tonight. The curtains were made of a heavy material that blocked all but a sliver of flashing light from outside. Hitler made his way over to the curtain and peeked out to see a parade passing four floors below.

He then turned his attention to the bed and, as his eyes adjusted once more, he slowly and cautiously crossed the room to it. There was someone in the bed, a man by all appearances. When an unusually bright light flashed past the window, he saw it was Winston Churchill.

Hitler pulled the Walther PPK he had been carrying for his own suicide and stepped closer to the bed. As he swung his arm up to a firing position, he accidentally brushed the lampshade of the lamp on the nightstand and sent it crashing to the floor.

Churchill awoke with a start and immediately sprang from his bed and reached for the drawer of the nightstand.

Hitler fired several shots, striking Churchill with each round. His nemesis collapsed to the floor, dead.

Hitler was elated and swung open the curtains, providing enough light by which to view the corpse of Churchill. With the light from outside shining in, Hitler could see that Churchill was clutching a book. Prying it from Churchill's lifeless hands, he read the title. *"My Struggle" by Winston Churchill.*

Puzzled, Hitler walked to the window and pulled back the curtains and sees that the buildings on the street were covered with Nazi flags and the people parading were wearing Nazi armbands.

THE ORACLE

He looked down and saw a newspaper on Churchill's desk. He picked up the paper and read the headline. It said that the forces of the Reich of Great Britain had the forces of the democracies of Italy, Japan and Germany on the run. Nothing could now stop the march of National Socialism!

PROCRASTINATION

"Step it up Amin," shouted the manager of the Manila movie theatre to the young usher. "You have only ten minutes to the next show," he yelled.

As Amin picked his way through the empty soda cups, candy wrappers, and popcorn strewn on the floor between the rows, he worked his way with the prized consignment in his refuse bag to one seat in the middle of the theater. The contents of his bag exhausted many man-hours of work to perfect.

Tonight would be its test.

He knew the blockbuster movie being shown, Pearl Harbor, would be sold out. He smiled to himself, realizing the irony of it all. All he had to do now was to choose a seat, and his task would be complete.

* * *

Alberto Espinoza had second thoughts about taking his young children to see a war movie. But he felt they should learn something about history, especially since the war portrayed ended with Filipino independence.

He and his two preteen sons had waited over an hour in line for the show but now they made their way to seats in the rapidly filling theater.

The boys wanted to sit in the middle of the theater to experience the full effect of the advertised realism of the movie. Seated with their drinks and snacks, the family settled in for an entertaining afternoon.

A few minutes into the movie, Alberto thought he heard a strange beeping sound, but he wasn't sure where it was coming from. He thought he heard it before, during the trailers, but now it seemed louder. He looked around, thinking perhaps some kid was playing with a game boy or some other electronic device, but no, there didn't appear to be anyone playing with anything.

When a quiet scene played in the movie, there it was again. Now it sounded as if it were right underneath him.

He stood up, kneeled down on the floor and peered under his seat. He saw in the dim light a tiny red blinking light and it seemed to be connected to a small box of some kind. He wondered what it could be. Then the red light stopped blinking and remained a steady beacon.

It was the last thing he saw.

There was a bright flash followed instantly by a blast of searing heat as the small box exploded into Alberto's face with a terrible roar.

* * *

"...and all toll, a dozen movie goers were killed and scores wounded," said the Filipino female newscaster on TV.

Amin, sitting in his small Manila hotel room located in the backwaters of the city, scratched his dark brown beard and looked over at his partner, Jamal. "The seat test worked perfectly. We're ready to move forward," he said in Filipino--his native language. "I go to Europe for the secondary plan. You complete the others here, then follow."

Amin stood up and turned off the TV, walked over to his brother and hugged him. "We'll see each other in paradise," he said, and left the room.

Outside, Amin pulled his collar up over the back of his neck against falling rain. He watched as a tall bearded Arab drove up to the curb in front him.

The lean Arab unlocked the passenger side door and Amin slid in beside him. "Your team is being gathered," he informed Amin. "Some are already in Europe and they are acquiring visas for America. You are to go to America first then to Germany to bring the rest of your team to the States. Understood?"

The young Amin nodded in response. He didn't question the change of itinerary. His role was to do as he was told.

"Good," the Arab said. "Now go. America will pay heavily for what they are doing to our Muslim brothers around the world."

Yes it will, thought Amin. *Yes it will.*

* * *

"Mrs. Ortega," the Officer said as he entered the interview room at the main Police Station in Manila. "I'm Detective Garcia and this is my partner Detective Santos."

The two detectives took seats across from Mrs. Ortega at the small interrogation table. They sat quietly, observing Mrs. Ortega for several seconds. It didn't take a detective to see she was nervous about having been brought to the station.

She was wringing the life out of her handkerchief as she sat waiting for the detectives to say something. She'd been brought in for questioning after it was learned that the suspect had stayed in the hotel where she was the chief desk clerk.

"Would you care for a cup of coffee?" Detective Garcia finally asked. She declined while continuing to wring the handkerchief.

"At this point, Mrs. Ortega, you are not under arrest or even a person under suspicion. We asked you here because we are hoping you will cooperate with us and provide us with information about one of the guests who recently stayed in the hotel. Do you think you could do that?"

"Yes. I will help you anyway I can. It might have been easier, though, if I were still at the hotel where I could have looked up answers in our guest book or in the hotel's notebook," Mrs. Garcia stated while still wringing the handkerchief.

"Mrs. Ortega," Detective Garcia said.

"You can call me, Maria," she interjected.

"Yes, of course, Maria," Detective Garcia began again. "What can you tell us about this man?" He slid a photo across the table for her to look at.

Maria took a moment to look closely at the picture before she answered. "His name is Abdul Samad. That's what his I.D. showed when he registered."

"That's the name he gave you?" asked Detective Santos.

"Yes, well…" Maria hesitated.

"Well what?" asked Garcia.

"Well, it is odd," Maria began. "He and his roommate…"

Santos interjected, "He had a roommate?" Then he and Garcia exchanged looks of concern.

"Yes. It's not unheard of. The room has two beds…"

"What about he and his roommate were strange?" Garcia interrupted this time and Maria gave him a nasty look, then continued.

"Anyway, I found it odd that he started to write his name on the guest registration form only to stop and tear it up after having written part of a name. It was as if he had forgotten his own name or how to spell it at least. The roommate didn't appear to be too bright."

"Are he and his roommate still staying at the hotel?" Santos asked while Detective Garcia flipped pages in his notebook looking for something.

"I'm not sure. They can check out at any time, but I do believe they've paid through to the end of the month. They look like students, but they never left their room. Each of them had a backpack, suitcase and a bag of books."

"What kind of books?" Detective Garcia asked.

"Oh, mostly science books."

"Did you happen to notice what kind of science books?" Garcia then asked.

"Well, I'm not positive, but I think I remember seeing Chemistry, something called Flow Dynamics and Electrical Theory, but I'm not positive. I just remember seeing those books lately."

"Okay, what else do you remember about them?" Santos inquired.

"They weren't very friendly. Oh, and they were secretive. The cleaning staff is very suspicious of them," Maria answered.

"Suspicious? Why?" Both Garcia and Santos asked at the same time.

"They double lock their door whenever they are inside the room. They have refused to allow us in to clean the room lately. One day about a week ago, I noticed the one calling himself Abdul had burned his hands somehow and he ignored me when I asked how he had gotten hurt. Plus, they were always carrying boxes in and out of their room. They refused any help from the bellboy."

Here eyebrows went up. "Oh, I almost forgot! They never eat in the hotel's restaurant or order room service. One of the two always goes out in the early evening to get fast food from a restaurant down the road."

The two detectives shared another glance, but neither one spoke for several moments - then Garcia asked, "What room are they in?"

"Room 305. It's on the third floor at the rear of the building."

"Thank you for your help," Santos said as he stood up and motioned for her to do the same. "We request that you don't return to your hotel right now for your own safety. Someone may have told these men about your being picked up for questioning. Do you understand?"

Maria Ortega nodded her head and continued to wring out her handkerchief.

* * *

Detectives Garcia and Santos waited in their unmarked sedan outside Maria Ortega's hotel. It wasn't exactly five star accommodations, and the neighborhood had long ago gone to seed. Down the block in a side alley sat one of the Manila Police Department's black SWAT vans with a crack team of eight SWAT officers inside.

Maria Ortega and the detectives were in a room overlooking the entrance of her hotel from across the street in an effort to have her point out either of the subjects as they exited the hotel.

The two detectives made small talk through the afternoon as they waited for one of the suspects to exit the hotel for their daily meal run. At seven-ten that evening, Maria confirmed the tall, dark-haired twenty something Pilipino was indeed the other man in room 305.

The man walked out of the building and turned left to a fast food place. He was inside for less than three minutes when he stepped out and turned towards the hotel, carrying the food in a white plastic bag flung over his shoulder.

"Let's move!" Garcia called out over the radio as he and Santos exited their car and began walking briskly towards Jamal. When they had closed to within thirty yards, Garcia yelled, "Halt!"

Jamal turned and saw the two men approaching. They were holding out their badges in one hand while holding guns in the other. He hesitated for a brief moment, then hurled his bag of food at them as he started to run.

Both Garcia and Santos ducked to avoid being hit by the flying food, then realized how stupid it was to duck a flying loaf of bread.

"Halt or we'll shoot!" Garcia yelled at the fleeing Jamal, who just kept on running and slipped into the hotel before either Detective could fire a clear shot.

"Shit! So much for an easy takedown," Santos groused as they ran to the hotel's front door. The eight men from the Department's SWAT Team joined them.

"Santos, take six men and go to the suspect's room. I'll take the other two and secure the back exits, then work our way to you. Remember, we want him alive if at all possible," Garcia reminded everyone.

Garcia made his way quickly around to the rear of the hotel as Santos and his team climbed the stairs to the third floor after locking down the elevators. Garcia entered the building via the rear entrance to the kitchen. As he stepped into the main dining room, he heard what sounded like an explosion, followed by dozens of gunshots.

Garcia and the two men with him raced up the stairs on the south side of the building. He took two steps at a time, as did the men behind him. As he climbed, he cursed himself for not taking the room, but something had told him the suspect would be coming out the back.

As they reached the third floor landing, the door burst open, and Jamal charged right into Garcia. The two men bowled head over heels down the short flight of stairs and landed with a thump on the landing halfway between the second and third floors.

Despite having the wind knocked out of him, Jamal continued to struggle with Garcia. The two SWAT officers had been knocked over in the collision as well and were just getting to their feet again when Jamal rolled away from Garcia, pulled his gun from some place Garcia hadn't seen and pointed it right at the detective.

Garcia instinctively swung his arm and knocked the gun from Jamal's bloody hand and then delivered a solid right punch to his jaw, temporarily disorienting him.

"Go secure the room and check on the others, I got this," Garcia bellowed as he wrenched Jamal's arms behind him to handcuff him.

Detective Santos and the rest of the SWAT team met the two SWAT team members at the door leading to the hallway.

Garcia sighed a sigh of relief, seeing no one had been injured. Then, once more, he ordered them to secure the room and took satisfaction from the fact that Jamal was moaning and groaning in pain.

Jamal, despite the pain and being handcuffed, tried several times to wiggle away from Garcia. Each time he tried, Garcia would yank his hands up off his back, causing Jamal to cry out in pain, which in turn brought a smile to Garcia's face.

"And you, scum bag," Garcia sneered over Jamal, "We're going to have a little talk."

* * *

Back at police headquarters, Santos reviewed the haul from the terrorist's hotel room. Before Jamal escaped from his room, he was able to set off a small firebomb that ignited the bomb making material and burned much of the documents and electronic files.

That was the dull blast heard by Garcia as he waited downstairs.

They discovered several floppy disks, memory sticks, and a laptop computer. The information contained on them had airline flight schedules, detonation times, and a list of operatives with code names such as "Zyed", "Majbos", "Markoa", "Mirqas" and "Obaid". Unfortunately, most of the other files were damaged and the information that was retrieved was not definitive as to the terrorist plot.

Included were the remains of a string of text files. The first string read, "Anyone who supports the U.S. Government are our targets. All Americans are responsible for their government's actions and thus support the U.S. foreign policies."

But the most disturbing find was a video file of one of the terrorists that fit the description of Jamal's roommate.

Garcia recognized it for what it was--the last testament of a suicide martyr.

"Look a this," he said to Santos, pointing to the video file playing on his desktop computer.

Santos looked at it and nodded. "This plot, whatever it may be, is well on its way."

"We better contact the U.S. Embassy," Garcia replied.

* * *

THE ORACLE

In Washington D.C., at the Headquarters of the FBI in the J. Edgar Hoover Building, the information from Manila had just arrived and was being analyzed by several levels of investigators.

"So what do you think?" FBI Special Agent Kathy Benson said, leaning against the doorjamb of the office and sipping on a Starbucks coffee.

Her partner, Michael Bowie, looked up and casually asked, "What's wrong with the coffee here at the office?"

"Not enough kick to it. I like the double shot of espresso I can add to my regular Mocha Grande. It gives me that octane boost to keep up with you big boys in the field," Benson retorted sarcastically. "So what do you think about this latest Intel?"

"Don't know for sure. The materials sent over by the Embassy certainly are compelling to a point but the information is incomplete. This could be just an elaborate ruse to get us out chasing our tails while they hit us some other place. If I have any say in how we proceed, I'll recommend that we proceed with caution and not to give this any more weight than any other lead. We don't even know if it's real. From where I'm sitting this is too good, too pat to be real."

"But it indicates that they are going to attack American based airlines," Benson offered.

"Perhaps, but let's look at the facts," Bowie began. "The bomb was planted under a movie seat. My guess is that they were testing to see how much damage the bomb configuration would do. When added to the information we have from the captured intel, it would appear that they were planning on attacking an airliner. Except there isn't any smoking gun or even a fizzled firecracker to confirm that idea." He frowned. "They could well be planning an attack on a crowded soccer stadium or a football or baseball stadium. How strong is the security at say, a Big Ten football game?"

"I suppose those are reasonable assumptions," Benson stated as she handed Bowie her coffee. "But they aren't talking about football schedules, start times or whether or not the game will be televised. They're talking about airplanes."

Bowie took a gulp of the coffee and let a satisfied, "Ahhh" escape his lips before asking, "Anything new on the APB we put out on the roommate of the dirt bag in Manila?"

"Nothing yet," Benson shared.

"Well, in the meantime," Bowie remarked, "we need to come up with some other ideas that might fit the information so we can stop these fanatics before they execute their plan. We need to find out the what, where and when all of this is going down. It could be today, tomorrow or next year for all we know. So let's earn our paycheck and find out, okay?"

* * *

Amin arrived at LAX in a somewhat altered state compared to how he looked when he left the Philippines. He was dressed in a custom made suit. He no longer had a beard, just a well-groomed mustache. He was dressed in a business suit, wearing wire-rimmed glasses and black slip-on shoes designed by Armani. To anyone who looked his way, he appeared to be a young professional. He was hoping to pass as an IT specialist.

His photo I.D. said his name was Miguel Adan.

Amin waited patiently in line at customs. When his turn came to present his passport and his luggage, the Customs Officer who checked him in was named Elliot Cameron. Amin was tired from the long flight and his patience was thin after having to stand in line for over an hour.

When he made eye contact, Officer Cameron noticed right away that Amin appeared to be irritated, and he decided to ask more extensive questions of the young Filipino businessman. Cameron learned from years of experience as a customs agent that it was the little things that made him suspicious——especially the stare with a hint of arrogance Amin gave Cameron.

"I.D., please." Officer Cameron politely demanded.

Amin fumbled with his wallet for several seconds before finally finding it and handing over his I.D.

Cameron looked over the I.D., carefully confirming that the picture matched and that there was a security watermark that showed up clearly when you looked at the I.D. from an angle. It was a good I.D. except for two very faint lines - one under the name and one running down the edge of the photo.

Cameron made a mental note of the two possible red flags and then moved on to question Amin's itinerary. "Why don't you have a return ticket to the Philippines?" Cameron asked.

Amin made it clear he resented the question with his snide reply. "Because I will be traveling on to other countries based upon the interview I have in Torrance tomorrow."

"You don't know where you're going after you leave the United States?" Cameron questioned.

"No, I don't. I may be going to France or Germany or Canada. It depends on the negotiations with my client and where my skills are needed most," Amin stated curtly.

Cameron mentally noted another red flag - short stay but no clear destination afterwards.

"I see. How quickly will you be moving on after your meeting tomorrow with your client?" Cameron asked.

"I suspect it will be within a day or two, three at most. I am an IT specialist and it's my job to trouble shoot problems with programming and fix it." Amin decided to try to speed things up by baffling the fool with bull crap.

"Where are you staying while in the country?" Officer Cameron then asked.

"I'm planning on staying at a local hotel or I might stay with a friend," Amin stated.

"What is your friend's name and address?" Cameron asked.

"What? Why do you need to know that?" Amin complained.

"Just answer the question, sir." Cameron remained professional, cold and indifferent.

"I don't know for sure. He lives in Anaheim," Amin stated after unknowingly making a face that suggested he was lying. Plus, it wasn't lost on Officer Cameron that Amin failed to provide the name of his friend. Cameron took his time looking over Amin's declaration.

When he had finished, he asked, "I see on your declaration page that you are declaring only six hundred dollars and no credit or debit cards. So how do you plan on covering the balance of your travel expenses?" Cameron watched Amin's face closely as he answered.

"My friend, ah…" Amin hesitated for a brief moment, then having figured out what to say next stated, "…is loaning me some money."

That was yet another red flag.

"Do you have a business card?" Cameron asked, catching Amin by surprise. It was lucky that his handler had thought of that and had given him two dozen business cards to bolster his new I.D.. Amin reached into his jacket pocket and pulled out a business card and handed it to Officer Cameron.

Cameron looked at the business card and noticed right away there wasn't an address on it, just a phone number with the city and country, Manila, Philippines. He also noted that the card didn't show the man's last name either.

"So, I can call this number and someone will answer saying it is…What is your company called?" Cameron asked.

"Miguel's IT Solutions. It is right there on the card," Amin snapped at Cameron. "Are you ready to check my bags yet?" Amin hoped to prod this jerk along.

"Do you work for your client as an employee or a sub-contractor?" Cameron asked.

"I am a subcontractor. I work for many companies in many countries. Can I go now?" Amin pressed.

That raised one more red flag in Cameron's mind. Why would someone embark on a trip without knowing where they were going? Cameron, under the guise of examining Amin's passport, took his time formulating his next few questions. When he knew how he wanted to trap this man in several lies, he proceeded.

"Where are you staying while in Los Angeles?" Cameron asked.

"I'm staying at the Embassy Suites in Torrance and yes, you can call them and they will say I have a reservation there for the next four nights.

I always book an extra night just in case," Amin stated as he wiped several beads of sweat off his forehead.

"What is the name of your contact person at your client's company?" Cameron asked next.

"What? Why would you need to know that?" Amin snapped at Cameron which was only making him more suspicious. "I demand to see your supervisor," Amin barked at the Custom's Officer.

Cameron signaled two of the officers guarding the Customs area and told them to watch Amin while he went to get his supervisor.

While waiting, Amin was looking all around and shifting about nervously.

Cameron entered the Customs office and walked up to the video console and waited until his Supervisor was ready to speak with him.

"So what's up with this one?" Gloria Adams asked now that she had reviewed the five minutes of tape involving Amin.

"He's extremely nervous. He's aggressive as well. Plus he is continually looking around as though he is worried about being followed or watched." Cameron said, sharing his observations.

"You haven't searched his luggage yet, have you?" Adams asked.

"No Mam, I've been questioning him. Just basic questions like how long is he staying in the country? Why doesn't he have a return ticket?

Who is he seeing while here? What does he do for a living? He had answers to every question but there are too many things about him that don't quite fit."

Adams leaned forward and began scrolling through the photos of the known undesirables on a priority watch list that the FBI had just issued the day before. She stopped and looked closely at a few photos, but continued on after a few brief moments with each one. That is, until she came across a photo of Abdul Samad, a Filipino last seen in Manila. Adams took a moment, looking hard at the photo. She then punched several keys on her keyboard in a flurry of motion.

The computer removed the Mustache, shorten the hair, added glasses and put the suspect in a suit. Adams and Cameron stood staring their mouths agape. The altered photo matched the man at the counter exactly, right down to the shape of his nose, eyes, and chin.

"Detain that man immediately. Treat his luggage as though it is explosive and call the FBI." Adams ordered.

Cameron came back out to the check in and did his best to appear as though he was totally at ease. "My supervisor is prepared to you see now. If you'll just follow me, I'll take you to her," Cameron stated as he nodded in a casual manner alerting the officers guarding Amin they would be taking him to detention.

"I've changed my mind. There's no reason to get all worked up over a little delay. I'm suffering from jet lag. That is all. I don't travel that well. I apologize for my rudeness. I know you're just doing your job."

Amin tried to avoid an even longer delay by apologizing, but it fell on deaf ears.

"No offense taken, Sir. But since the request was made, I really must insist that you come with me," Cameron stated, and the two burly officers grabbed Amin, quickly ushering him out of the public area and to the detention holding cell.

* * *

"He'll be at Dulles within the hour," FBI agent Kathy Benson said as she checked her watch for the time.

"If you keep checking on the time you'll wear that watch out," Bowie joked. "We'll pick him up and take him straight to Tactical Interrogation. Then I'll file my report with the Director from there."

"Tactical Interrogation? When did that reopen?" Benson asked.

"It never closed," Bowie remarked casually. "The story that it did close was strictly a red herring for the media and a couple of watch dog groups. The public players were transferred to other programs and the building was refurbished to appear as though it was being redeveloped into office space."

"So what will happen at T.I.?" Benson asked.

"If I have to spell it out for you, Kathy, you really don't want to know," Bowie stated emphatically.

* * *

Bowie and Benson met the plane carrying Amin off to the far side of the airport in the private aviation section. The ten-passenger Lear Jet rolled to a stop in front of an unmarked hanger and two unmarked cars pulled up alongside. Minutes later, four burly special agents hustled a shackled Amin off the plane. It was clear by his stagger Amin had already been questioned at length about his involvement in the new plot.

Bowie and Benson stepped over next to the car Amin was loaded into and introduced themselves to the four special agents from the L.A. Office. After an exchange of pleasantries, Bowie and Benson were informed about the suspect's questioning in route from L.A., and it wasn't promising.

"We weren't able to get much out of him. We even went so far as to threaten to water board him and nothing," the lead agent from L.A. stated.

"So why didn't you water board him?" Benson asked.

"We weren't authorized to do it," the lead agent replied.

"Well now that we have him here," Bowie stated, "I think the gloves will come off. He gets an all expense paid trip to Tactical Interrogation. They'll get the information out of him."

"Good luck, he's a real arrogant bastard," the lead agent stated as he boarded the plane for the trip back to L.A.

* * *

The trip across town and then out into the countryside between D.C. and the Chesapeake Bay took nearly an hour. They drove up to what appeared to be an abandoned house that overlooked the water. As soon as they came to a stop, four men raced from the house, grabbed Amin, and hauled him out of the backseat of the car.

The house at one time had been painted white and had a large flower garden inside the half circle driveway directly in front of the main entry door. Swiftly four men exited the house, and they returned dragging Amin by the shackles. To underscore the severity of the situation that Amin was now in, Bowie and Benson heard a scream as the door closed behind the four men carrying Amin.

Amin had been assigned the status of "Enemy Combatant" which allowed the FBI free rein when questioning subjects regarding terrorism. It was not invoked lightly for it is extreme and brutal.

So if Amin were to suffer, no matter how great his suffering might be, it was not a concern for Bowie. We didn't start this war, they did, and the rules of war were simple – all's fair.

* * *

Bowie took a sip of his fourth latte and looked at his watch. They had been at this Starbuck's for over three hours. He cursed Amin and his stubbornness. He randomly thought he might never get to sleep a full eight hours ever again.

Benson had been dozing while Bowie reread the file on the supposedly imminent attacks and still he didn't see it.

He had just taken a gulp of that latte when Benson stirred. Oh, how he envied her ability to take catnaps and feel refreshed after having done so. A catnap for Bowie was an exercise in futility. Short naps always left him feeling more drained than before he dozed off.

Benson yawned and took a sip of her double espresso mocha latte and asked, "How much longer to you think it'll be?"

"As long as it takes to get Amin to tell us everything he knows."

"Could be a long night." Benson smirked at Bowie, who faked a smile and quickly resorted to just looking tired.

"Did you notice the bastard's defiant attitude? He was all trussed up in shackles and yet he acted no more concerned than if he was going to a coffee klatch," Bowie pointed out, then waved at the counter girl, pointing at his cup. "He'll be hard to break," he added as the waitress made her way to their table.

Bowie had been right. It was early morning the next day before the interrogators were able to obtain any actionable information. His phone rang just as he was about to order breakfast vibrating across the tabletop as if it had suddenly been blessed with a life of its own. Bowie scooped it up and answered it.

He listened for a few brief moments, then hung up and said to Benson, "Amin's talking. It's not complete details. Either he was able to hide some of the information or he just doesn't know it. We need to get over there ASAP."

Bowie threw forty bucks on the table, silently cursing the cost of a caffeine habit, then he and Benson headed out to the car.

They drove back over to the safe house and were quickly ushered inside. There, in the center of what had been the living room, sat Amin drenched in sweat and clothed only in his torn and piss stained Jockey shorts. He was handcuffed to a chair, his whole body shaking uncontrollably. He was a mess with blood, sweat, and tears running down his face. His hair was in knots and dozens of obvious welts covered the exposed portions of his body.

Amin's condition mattered little to Bowie as he strode across the room, asking the interrogator, "How did you manage to break him?"

The FBI interrogator was a huge, muscular man with a crooked nose and sharp steely eyes. He pulled Bowie off to the side, out of earshot of Amin, and explained how he gained Amin's cooperation.

"One of my men masqueraded as a Mossad agent and we told that piece of shit if he didn't cooperate we'd send him to Israel so the Mossad could further interrogate him. That changed his mind real fast and he started singing like a canary."

The interrogator told Bowie and Benson that Amin was part of a terrorist plot to hijack airlines and/or bomb them. And it pointed to the Pacific. From what they could gather from Amin and the final analyzes of the intelligence garnered from the materials at Amin's hotel room,

Amin was to meet others in the plot in Germany and, from there, to the U.S.

But Amin also stated that some of the soon-to-be terrorists were already in the U.S. He and the group from Germany were to join them.

"That SOB gave up names," the interrogator noted. "We can use that information to track down those in Germany and pick them up."

"If he gave us the *right* names," Bowie frowned. "These bastards change their names from their original ones when they decide to become martyrs."

Benson nodded. "If we think the Pacific is the target, they should be looking to travel to the West Coast."

"Yes. Makes sense," Bowie replied. "Let's get on these names. With some luck we can pick up one of them here in the east and get him to identify some of others before they leave for the West Coast. Maybe we can break up the whole plot."

* * *

Mohammed Yousef, was high on cocaine and drinking heavily at the Mustang Strip Club in Washington D.C., enjoying his last hours before martyrdom. He and his friend and fellow martyr, Satam al Suqami, were sitting off to the side of the main dance floor out of the limelight, enjoying lap dances from well-endowed topless blonde women.

The woman who was dancing for Mohammad was working it for all she had because Mohammed was flashing around hundred-dollar bills as if he had a printing press in the trunk of his car.

"That'll be another hundred, baby, if you'd like to do more," the woman breathed lustfully as she unbuttoned his shirt and ran her hand across his bare chest.

Yousef was conflicted as he struggled to justify his behavior. He was feeling both lust and contempt for this woman. With her wild gyrations, she was causing his sexual lust and desire to boil to the surface. Yet, those same gyrations reminded him of his religious teachings, thus contempt raged just below the surface. The harder the woman tried to excite him, the more he was feeling contempt for her and the decadent infidels that permeate the American culture.

He took a snort of cocaine and washed it down with another shot of Jack Daniel's as the woman ground her buttocks against his lap, moving rhythmically to the music. Between the flashing lights, loud music, cocaine and alcohol. He could feel himself slipping away. The room was spinning, and his mind was racing in nonsensical circles. He reached out to touch the woman, now shaking her naked breast before his face, and the moment he touched her, it was as if he had been struck by lightning.

Suddenly, he was filled with remorse and guilt - swept away on a wave of paranoia that enforced the belief he had somehow given away his chance at the seventy-two virgins as well as paradise itself.

He suddenly grabbed her breast roughly and squeezed until the woman recoiled and screamed for a bouncer, which sent Mohammad into a frenzied panic attack.

Yousef then grabbed the woman by the throat with both hands to silence her as he bolted up and out of his chair. With his strength intensified by the drugs and alcohol, he lifted her two feet off the floor and began tightening his grip around her neck, cutting off her air. He stood there squeezing her throat while screaming in Arabic.

The woman was flinging her arms and legs, kicking and hitting Mohammed, but it was useless. He was so drugged he felt nothing and he was aware only of the fact that the woman had tempted him into betraying his faith and for that she must die.

She struggled to scream, for Mohammad was crushing her windpipe. In her last desperate act, she began clawing at his face, sinking her nails in deeply and peeling long strips of skin from his face.

But he was unyielding, relentless.

At the edge of consciousness, the stripper felt his grip loosen and suddenly she was pulled away from him. She fell to the floor gasping for air. As she lay struggling to breathe, she looked up and saw two bouncers wrestling with the bastard on the floor a few feet away.

The wad of hundred-dollar bills Mohammad had was now on the floor under the chair where he had been seated. She reached out scooped up the cash and crawled several feet away before one of the other customers came to her rescue and helped her up to her feet. She then staggered into the dressing room and slammed the door behind her.

Mohammad was beaten black and blue by the bouncers and once they had him restrained, the stripper returned wearing just robe and heavy-duty boots. She first spit on him, which further enraged him, but the bouncers had him held down too well for him to continue his attack.

As a parting gift, the stripper stepped down alongside of Mohammad's prone body and stomped the man's groin several times before stomping off back to the dressing room.

Through clenched teeth, Mohammad screamed "Allah Akbar" and then cursed America and the whore of a woman who tempted him. He yelled loudly that America would soon face its punishment for its crimes against Islam.

Later on, when the local police were taking statements about the incident, witnesses shared about how Mohammad's friend had run out the moment Mohammad had grabbed the woman.

* * *

"Was that all he said?" special agent Bowie asked the detective at the Washington, D.C. downtown Metro Police Precinct house. Bowie had the phone on speaker so that special agent Benson could hear as well. The clock on the wall said it was five a.m.

"He was screaming a bunch of stuff in Arabic or Farsi or whatever that no one in the place was able to understand," said the D.C. Detective.

"Near the end of his rant he screamed, 'Allah Akbar', and something about how America was going to be punished by the hand of God."

"Do you have anything else?" Bowie asked, thinking it was like pulling teeth getting information out of the local yokel.

"Only that he cried out for someone to help him, but like I said, his buddy bolted the moment this Mohammad guy freaked out. One of the witnesses said they thought they heard him call out a name but it isn't like any name I've ever heard. She said he called him Zyed."

"Zyed, are you sure that was it?" Bowie asked.

"Yeah, I wrote it down in my notes."

"Did anyone follow this Zyed out the door?"

"Not that anyone could remember. By the time we got here he was long gone and this guy Mohammad was pinned to the floor by two big bouncers. His face looked like someone took a gardening claw to it. He was a bloody mess."

"Thank you, Detective. We'll have a couple of agents come by and pick him up ASAP," Bowie stated, then hung up.

"What do you think? Is he part of this plot?" Benson asked.

I think this Mohammad Yousef and his partner are two of the terrorists that have come in from Germany. Zyed was one of the code names on Amin's zip drives. I'm thinking now that the names aren't code words at all, just names of his co-conspirators." Bowie stood up and slipped on his suit coat. "Let's get a move on. I'm afraid what's going down will be today."

"Last night was his final send off before martyrdom?" Benson asked.

"I'd bet your money it was."

* * *

Thirty minutes later, Special agents Bowie and Benson were at the downtown Metro Police Precinct in D.C. about to walk into Detective Bisbee's office.

"Glad you're here," Bisbee stated as they stepped through his office door, "We got the bastard."

"How's that?" Bowie asked.

"We've done a preliminary search of the suspect's hotel room. Did I mention the DA is seeking attempted murder? Oh well, not important. We found this." Bisbee handed a small packet of papers to Bowie.

Bowie took a quick look at them and handed them to Benson with a smile, "Airline tickets and boarding passes."

"And we have the name of this guy Zyed," Bisbee added. "He left his martyrdom tape in the hotel room to be found later after the fact. He announces his real name. I bet he's on the flight manifest under one or the other." Bisbee crowed with self-pride.

"Good work, Detective," Benson stated.

Bisbee's mood turned grim as he said, "The only problem is, the flight leaves in fifteen minutes."

Bowie and Benson stood up quickly thanking Bisbee as they rushed out of his office and began trotting through the precinct house. As they ran, Bowie flipped open his cell phone and made a call.

A few seconds later, he was talking to his supervisor, Clarence Claypool. "That's right. The flight leaves from Dulles in less than fifteen minutes - probably more like ten." Bowie explained. "Call the FAA and see what we can do to stop the flight."

Claypool replied, "There's not enough time. Besides, why give a couple of hundred passengers a bad day by canceling the flight. We know who this guy is and we can pick up him, and anyone who meets him, in L.A."

Bowie protested. "But at least try, sir."

"Look, Bowie. You did a yeoman's job on this. You and Benson will get a commendation. Now go post your final report and take a few days off. You two earned it."

"Yes, sir. Thank you, sir." Bowie hung up and turned to Benson. "That's it. We're out of it. The L.A. office will handled it from here."

"So we just wait," Benson remarked.

Bowie shrugged his shoulders.

"Well, I need to get me some breakfast." She tugged on Bowie's sleeve. "Comin' along?"

"No. I need to file our report. Let's do lunch later."

Benson smiled, nodded and walked off.

* * *

When Bowie returned to his office, he made himself a cup of coffee. Satisfied, mixed with some milk to just the right shade of tan, he took a sip and thought about his supervisor's act of procrastination.

Maybe his boss was right. Where else could the terrorists go? Can't get off a non-stop flight in midair.

He placed his coffee down, put on his headset, and spoke his final report into his computer.

Case Report Number: Alpha Tango Six Zero Seven.

Re: Pacific Terror Plot.

From: Special Agent Michael Bowie.

Time: 7:46 AM Eastern Standard Time.

Date: Tuesday, 11 September 2001…

214

"Dinner's ready, gentlemen," Helen announced as she entered the living room. "I've also prepared a room for you down the hall, young man."

"Thank you, I'm sure it will be far better than I'm used to," I stated as I rose and followed her to the dinner table.

"Oh, I wouldn't go that far, but it's clean and dry." Helen stated with pride.

The three of us ate dinner while keeping the conversation focused on small talk like places I've lived, the car I was driving, how long I'd be in Texas and so on.

When we'd finished, Helen cleared the table and wouldn't hear of me helping. She said goodnight and told me she'd see me in the morning. She admonished Jeb not to keep me up too late and kissed his cheek as she left.

Jeb huffed and waited to be sure Helen wasn't going to come back, having forgotten to say something she thought was important. As soon as he was sure we were alone again, he lit another hand-rolled cigarette. "I'll show you to your room. I have to check on the horses before I can call it a night."

Old Jeb led me down a long hallway to a room across from the guest bathroom - as Helen called it. Once I was inside the room, Jeb mumbled *good night around his rollie and closed the door. For a moment, I thought he might have locked me in.*

I waited until I heard the sound of the front door open and close before I ventured over to the bedroom door and tried the handle. It was open.

I peeked into the hallway and couldn't see much of anything. It was pretty dark. With the lights in the house off, the only light source was the lightning flashes that occurred every few seconds. I guess the storm was still raging, but it had drifted off a few miles so that despite the lightning flashing in the distance, there wasn't much thunder.

As soon as I knew he was gone, I quietly left the room and made my way to the kitchen, thinking the way down to the cellar was there.

I was right. I found a door and it opened to a set of stairs leading down into a dark hollow. I searched the wall with my hand, looking for a light switch, and found one just by the door. I clicked it on and descended into a cold, musky basement.

I made my way over boxes, crates and trunks of years of personal treasures, squinting my eyes in the dim light. Then I noticed something long and slivery protruding from behind several of the boxes.

Found it!

I cleared away the boxes and saw, what Jeb had called a spaceship, was in reality a four-foot long three-foot around cylinder.

THE ORACLE

I was excited.

Now I'll find out what the meanings of those slides were!

I kneeled down next to the cylinder and searched for a way to open it. After a few hectic minutes, I found a seam along a panel that showed the promise of an entry. I pushed on the panel, and with a slight hiss, it popped open!

Thrilled, I pulled the panel back and surveyed the cylinder's contents. There were several items in the cylinder—-some I could recognize, but others not. I was puzzled by some of the items with strange names on them, like iPad and iPhone.

After pulling all the items out of the cylinder, my hand hit some kind of lever on the underside. I pushed on it and, to my surprise, an image of a man projected on the basement wall—-and he started to talk.

But mid-way through the capsule's diatribe, the man ceased, and the image disappeared.

I sat on the cold damp floor, contemplating what I had just seen and heard.

The man said the cylinder was a time capsule. Not one that was buried by a society of the past wishing to inform those in the future of its culture, but a time capsule that was sent from a future society back into time to inform those in the past of what the future will behold.

Suddenly, the mystery of the slides dawned on me. I ran upstairs, entered the living room, and grabbed the box of slides. I open it and unceremoniously dumped all the slides onto the coffee table. At the very bottom of the box, wedged in sideways, was another slide. I picked it up and placed it in the stereoscope viewer--and was met with a surprise.

This forgotten slide proceeded to run a 'trailer' advertising the entire previous story slides and others, ending with a blurb that stated in no uncertain terms:

Copyrighted 2050 by LucusFilms, Incorporated. All rights reserved. Unauthorized reproduction of this material is punishable by 250,000 Bitcoins and five years in a community rehabilitation program.